William Faulkner

BIG WOODS

William Faulkner, one of the greatest writers of the twentieth century, was born in New Albany, Mississippi, on September 25, 1897. He published his first book, *The Marble Faun*, a collection of poems, in 1924, but it is as a literary chronicler of life in the Deep South — particularly in the fictional Yoknapatawpha County, the setting for several of his novels — that he is most highly regarded. In such novels as *Sanctuary* (1931), *The Hamlet* (1940), *The Town* (1957), and *The Mansion* (1959), he explored the full range of post–Civil War Southern life, focusing both on the personal histories of his characters (especially members of the Snopes family) and on the moral uncertainties of an increasingly dissolute society. His other novels include *The Sound and the Fury* (1929), *As I Lay Dying* (1930), *Light in August* (1932), *Absalom, Absalom!* (1936), *The Unvanquished* (1938), *Intruder in the Dust* (1948), *Requiem for a Nun* (1951), *A Fable* (1954), and *The Reivers* (1962). For the latter two books, he was awarded the Pulitzer Prize. He also wrote several volumes of short stories as well as collections of poems and essays.

In combining the use of symbolism with a stream-of-consciousness technique, he created a new approach to the writing of fiction. In 1949, he was awarded the Nobel Prize for Literature.

William Faulkner died in Byhalia, Mississippi, on July 6, 1962.

VINTAGE

INTERNATIONAL

BOOKS BY *William Faulkner*

AVAILABLE FROM VINTAGE

Absalom, Absalom!

As I Lay Dying

Big Woods

Collected Stories

A Fable

Flags in the Dust

Go Down, Moses

The Hamlet

Intruder in the Dust

Knight's Gambit

Light in August

The Mansion

Pylon

The Reivers

Requiem for a Nun

Sanctuary

Selected Letters of William Faulkner

The Sound and the Fury

Three Famous Short Novels:
Spotted Horses, Old Man, The Bear

The Town

The Uncollected Stories of William Faulkner

The Unvanquished

The Wild Palms

Big Woods

BIG WOODS

The Hunting Stories

BY WILLIAM FAULKNER

VINTAGE INTERNATIONAL

VINTAGE BOOKS

A DIVISION OF RANDOM HOUSE, INC.

NEW YORK

FIRST VINTAGE INTERNATIONAL EDITION, MAY 1994

Library of Congress Cataloging-in-Publication Data
Faulkner, William, 1897–1962.
Big woods: the hunting stories / by William Faulkner. — 1st
Vintage international ed.
p. cm.
ISBN 0-679-75252-8
1. Hunting stories, American.   I. Title.
PS3511.A86B54   1994
813'.52 — dc20   94-5687
CIP

Manufactured in the United States of America
10   9   8   7   6   5   4   3

We never always saw eye to eye
but we were always
looking at the same thing

CONTENTS

Big Woods

Mississippi:

*The rich deep black alluvial soil which would grow
cotton taller than the head of a man on a horse, already
one jungle one brake one impassable density of brier
and cane and vine interlocking the soar of gum and
cypress and hickory and pinoak and ash, printed now
by the tracks of unalien shapes—bear and deer and
panthers and bison and wolves and alligators and the
myriad smaller beasts, and unalien men to name them
too perhaps—the (themselves) nameless though
recorded predecessors who built the mounds to escape the
spring floods and left their meagre artifacts: the obsolete
and the dispossessed, dispossessed by those who were
dispossessed in turn because they too were obsolete: the
wild Algonquian, Chickasaw and Choctaw and Natchez
and Pascagoula, peering in virgin astonishment down*

from the tall bluffs at a Chippeway canoe bearing three
Frenchmen—and had barely time to whirl and look
behind him at ten and then a hundred and then a thousand
Spaniards come overland from the Atlantic Ocean:
a tide, a wash, a thrice flux-and-ebb of motion so rapid
and quick across the land's slow alluvial chronicle as to
resemble the limber flicking of the magician's one hand
before the other holding the deck of inconstant cards: the
Frenchman for a moment, then the Spaniard for perhaps
two, then the Frenchman for another two and then
the Spaniard again for another and then the Frenchman
for that one last second, half-breath; because then came
the Anglo-Saxon, the pioneer, the tall man, roaring with
Protestant scripture and boiled whisky, Bible and jug
in one hand and (like as not) a native tomahawk in the
other, brawling, turbulent not through viciousness but
simply because of his over-revved glands; uxorious and
polygamous: a married invincible bachelor, dragging
his gravid wife and most of the rest of his mother-in-law's
family behind him into the trackless infested forest,
spawning that child as like as not behind the barricade
of a rifle-crotched log mapless leagues from nowhere
and then getting her with another one before reaching his
final itch-footed destination, and at the same time
scattering his ebullient seed in a hundred dusky bellies
through a thousand miles of wilderness; innocent and
gullible, without bowels for avarice or compassion or

forethought either, changing the face of the earth: felling
a tree which took two hundred years to grow, in order to
extract from it a bear or a capful of wild honey;

Obsolete too: still felling the two-hundred-year-old tree
when the bear and the wild honey were gone and there
was nothing in it any more but a raccoon or a possum
whose hide was worth at the most two dollars, turning
the earth into a howling waste from which he would be
the first to vanish, not even on the heels but synchronous
with the slightly darker wild men whom he had
dispossessed, because, like them, only the wilderness could
feed and nourish him; and so disappeared, strutted his
roaring eupeptic hour, and was no more, leaving his
ghost, pariah and proscribed, scriptureless now and
armed only with the highwayman's, the murderer's,
pistol, haunting the fringes of the wilderness which he
himself had helped to destroy, because the river towns
marched now recessional south by south along the
processional bluffs: St Louis, Paducah, Memphis, Helena,
Vicksburg, Natchez, Baton Rouge, peopled by men with
mouths full of law, in broadcloth and flowered waistcoats,
who owned Negro slaves and Empire beds and
buhl cabinets and ormolu clocks, who strolled and
smoked their cigars along the bluffs beneath which in
the shanty and flatboat purlieus he rioted out the last of
his doomed evening, losing his worthless life again and

again to the fierce knives of his drunken and worthless kind—this in the intervals of being pursued and harried in his vanishing avatars of Harpe and Hare and Mason and Murrel, either shot on sight or hoicked, dragged out of what remained of his secret wilderness haunts along the overland Natchez trace (one day someone brought a curious seed into the land and inserted it into the earth, and now vast fields of white not only covered the waste places which with his wanton and heedless axe he had made, but were effacing, thrusting back the wilderness even faster than he had been able to, so that he barely had a screen for his back when, crouched in his thicket, he glared at his dispossessor in impotent and incredulous and uncomprehending rage) into the towns to his formal apotheosis in a courtroom and then a gallows or the limb of a tree;

Because those days were gone, the old brave innocent tumultuous eupeptic tomorrowless days; the last broadhorn and keelboat (Mike Fink was a legend; soon even the grandfathers would no longer claim to remember him, and the river hero was now the steamboat gambler wading ashore in his draggled finery from the towhead where the captain had marooned him) had been sold piecemeal for firewood in Chartres and Toulouse and Dauphine street, and Choctaw and Chickasaw braves, in short hair and overalls and armed with mule-whips in

*place of war-clubs and already packed up to move west
to Oklahoma, watched steamboats furrowing even the
shallowest and remotest wilderness streams where tumbled
gently to the motion of the paddle-wheels, the gutted
rock-weighted bones of Hare's and Mason's murderees;
a new time, a new age, millennium's beginning; one vast
single net of commerce webbed and veined the
midcontinent's fluvial embracement; New Orleans,
Pittsburgh, and Fort Bridger, Wyoming, were suburbs
one to the other, inextricable in destiny; men's mouths
were full of law and order, all men's mouths were round
with the sound of money; one unanimous golden
affirmation ululated the nation's boundless immeasurable
forenoon: profit plus regimen equals security: a nation of
commonwealths; that crumb, that dome, that gilded
pustule, that Idea risen now, suspended like a balloon or
a portent or a thundercloud above what used to be
wilderness, drawing, holding the eyes of all: Mississippi.*

1

THE
BEAR

1. There was a man and a dog too this time. Two
beasts, counting Old Ben, the bear, and two men, counting
Boon Hogganbeck, in whom some of the same blood ran
which ran in Sam Fathers, even though Boon's was a plebeian strain of it and only Sam and Old Ben and the mongrel
Lion were taintless and incorruptible.

He was sixteen. For six years now he had been a man's
hunter. For six years now he had heard the best of all talking. It was of the wilderness, the big woods, bigger and
older than any recorded document:—of white man fatuous
enough to believe he had bought any fragment of it, of
Indian ruthless enough to pretend that any fragment of it
had been his to convey; bigger than Major de Spain and the
scrap he pretended to, knowing better; older than old
Thomas Sutpen of whom Major de Spain had had it and
who knew better; older even than old Ikkemotubbe, the
Chickasaw chief, of whom old Sutpen had had it and who
knew better in his turn. It was of the men, not white nor
black nor red but men, hunters, with the will and hardi-
hood to endure and the humility and skill to survive, and
the dogs and the bear and deer juxtaposed and reliefed
against it, ordered and compelled by and within the wilderness in the ancient and unremitting contest according to
the ancient and immitigable rules which voided all regrets
and brooked no quarter—the best game of all, the best of
all breathing and forever the best of all listening, the voices
quiet and weighty and deliberate for retrospection and recollection and exactitude among the concrete trophies—the

racked guns and the heads and skins—in the libraries of town houses or the offices of plantation houses or (and best of all) in the camps themselves where the intact and still-warm meat yet hung, the men who had slain it sitting before the burning logs on hearths when there were houses and hearths or about the smoky blazing of piled wood in front of stretched tarpaulins when there were not. There was always a bottle present, so that it would seem to him that those fine fierce instants of heart and brain and courage and wiliness and speed were concentrated and distilled into that brown liquor which not women, not boys and children, but only hunters drank, drinking not of the blood they spilled but some condensation of the wild immortal spirit, drinking it moderately, humbly even, not with the pagan's base and baseless hope of acquiring thereby the virtues of cunning and strength and speed but in salute to them. Thus it seemed to him on this December morning not only natural but actually fitting that this should have begun with whisky.

He realised later that it had begun long before that. It had already begun on that day when he first wrote his age in two ciphers and his cousin McCaslin brought him for the first time to the camp, the big woods, to earn for himself from the wilderness the name and state of hunter provided he in his turn were humble and enduring enough. He had already inherited then, without ever having seen it, the big old bear with one trap-ruined foot that in an area almost a hundred miles square had earned for himself a name, a definite designation like a living man:—the long legend of corn-cribs broken down and rifled, of shoats and grown pigs and even calves carried bodily into the woods and de-

voured and traps and deadfalls overthrown and dogs
mangled and slain and shotgun and even rifle shots delivered
at point-blank range yet with no more effect than so many
peas blown through a tube by a child—a corridor of wreck-
age and destruction beginning back before the boy was
born, through which sped, not fast but rather with the ruthless and irresistible deliberation of a locomotive, the shaggy
tremendous shape. It ran in his knowledge before he
ever saw it. It loomed and towered in his dreams before he
even saw the unaxed woods where it left its crooked print,
shaggy, tremendous, red-eyed, not malevolent but just big,
too big for the dogs which tried to bay it, for the horses
which tried to ride it down, for the men and the bullets they
fired into it; too big for the very country which was its con-
stricting scope. It was as if the boy had already divined what
his senses and intellect had not encompassed yet: that
doomed wilderness whose edges were being constantly and
punily gnawed at by men with plows and axes who feared
it because it was wilderness, men myriad and nameless even
to one another in the land where the old bear had earned a
name, and through which ran not even a mortal beast but
an anachronism indomitable and invincible out of an old
dead time, a phantom, epitome and apotheosis of the old
wild life which the little puny humans swarmed and hacked
at in a fury of abhorrence and fear like pygmies about the
ankles of a drowsing elephant;—the older bear, solitary,
indomitable, and alone; widowered childless and absolved
of mortality—old Priam reft of his old wife and outlived all
his sons.

Still a child, with three years then two years then one year yet before he too could make one of them, each November he would watch the wagon containing the dogs and the bedding and food and guns and his cousin McCaslin and Tennie's Jim and Sam Fathers too until Sam moved to the camp to live, depart for the Big Bottom, the big woods. To him, they were going not to hunt bear and deer but to keep yearly rendezvous with the bear which they did not even intend to kill. Two weeks later they would return, with no trophy, no skin. He had not expected it. He had not even feared that it might be in the wagon this time with the other skins and heads. He did not even tell himself that in three years or two years or one year more he would be present and that it might even be his gun. He believed that only after he had served his apprenticeship in the woods which would prove him worthy to be a hunter, would he even be permitted to distinguish the crooked print, and that even then for two November weeks he would merely make another minor one, along with his cousin and Major de Spain and General Compson and Walter Ewell and Boon and the dogs which feared to bay it and the shotguns and rifles which failed even to bleed it, in the yearly pageant-rite of the old bear's furious immortality.

His day came at last. In the surrey with his cousin and Major de Spain and General Compson he saw the wilderness through a slow drizzle of November rain just above the ice point as it seemed to him later he always saw it or at least always remembered it—the tall and endless wall of dense November woods under the dissolving afternoon and

the year's death, sombre, impenetrable (he could not even
discern yet how, at what point they could possibly hope to
enter it even though he knew that Sam Fathers was waiting
there with the wagon), the surrey moving through the
skeleton stalks of cotton and corn in the last of open country, the last trace of man's puny gnawing at the immemorial
flank, until, dwarfed by that perspective into an almost
ridiculous diminishment, the surrey itself seemed to have
ceased to move (this too to be completed later, years later,
after he had grown to a man and had seen the sea) as a
solitary small boat hangs in lonely immobility, merely toss-
ing up and down, in the infinite waste of the ocean while the
water and then the apparently impenetrable land which it
nears without appreciable progress, swings slowly and opens
the widening inlet which is the anchorage. He entered it.
Sam was waiting, wrapped in a quilt on the wagon seat
behind the patient and steaming mules. He entered his no-
vitiate to the true wilderness with Sam beside him as he had
begun his apprenticeship in miniature to manhood after the
rabbits and such with Sam beside him, the two of them
wrapped in the damp, warm, Negro-rank quilt while the
wilderness closed behind his entrance as it had opened
momentarily to accept him, opening before his advance-
ment as it closed behind his progress, no fixed path the
wagon followed but a channel nonexistent ten yards ahead
of it and ceasing to exist ten yards after it had passed, the
wagon progressing not by its own volition but by attrition
of their intact yet fluid circumambience, drowsing, earless,
almost lightless.

It seemed to him that at the age of ten he was witnessing his own birth. It was not even strange to him. He had experienced it all before, and not merely in dreams. He saw the camp—a paintless six-room bungalow set on piles above the spring high-water—and he knew already how it was going to look. He helped in the rapid orderly disorder of their establishment in it and even his motions were familiar to him, foreknown. Then for two weeks he ate the coarse, rapid food—the shapeless sour bread, the wild strange meat, venison and bear and turkey and coon which he had never tasted before—which men ate, cooked by men who were hunters first and cooks afterward; he slept in harsh sheetless blankets as hunters slept. Each morning the gray of dawn found him and Sam Fathers on the stand, the crossing, which had been allotted him. It was the poorest one, the most barren. He had expected that; he had not dared yet to hope even to himself that he would even hear the running dogs this first time. But he did hear them. It was on the third morning—a murmur, sourceless, almost indistinguishable, yet he knew what it was although he had never before heard that many dogs running at once, the murmur swelling into separate and distinct voices until he could call the five dogs which his cousin owned from among the others. "Now," Sam said, "slant your gun up a little and draw back the hammers and then stand still."

But it was not for him, not yet. The humility was there; he had learned that. And he could learn the patience. He was only ten, only one week. The instant had passed. It seemed to him that he could actually see the deer, the buck, smoke-colored, elongated with speed, vanished, the woods, the gray solitude still ringing even when the voices of the dogs had died away; from far away across the sombre woods and the gray half-liquid morning there came two shots. "Now let your hammers down," Sam said.

He did so. "You knew it too," he said.

"Yes," Sam said. "I want you to learn how to do when you didn't shoot. It's after the chance for the bear or the deer has done already come and gone that men and dogs get killed."

"Anyway, it wasn't him," the boy said. "It wasn't even a bear. It was just a deer."

"Yes," Sam said, "it was just a deer."

Then one morning, it was in the second week, he heard the dogs again. This time before Sam even spoke he readied the too-long, too-heavy, man-size gun as Sam had taught him, even though this time he knew the dogs and the deer were coming less close than ever, hardly within hearing even. They didn't sound like any running dogs he had ever heard before even. Then he found that Sam, who had taught him first of all to cock the gun and take position where he could see best in all directions and then never to move again, had himself moved up beside him. "There," he said. "Listen." The boy listened, to no ringing chorus strong and fast on a free scent but a moiling yapping an octave too high and with something more than indecision and even abjectness in it which he could not yet recognise, reluctant, not even moving very fast, taking a long time to pass out of hearing, leaving even then in the air that echo of thin and almost human hysteria, abject, almost humanly grieving, with this time nothing ahead of it, no sense of a fleeing unseen smoke-colored shape. He could hear Sam breathing at his shoulder. He saw the arched curve of the old man's inhaling nostrils.

"It's Old Ben!" he cried, whispering.

Sam didn't move save for the slow gradual turning of his head as the voices faded on and the faint steady rapid arch and collapse of his nostrils. "Hah," he said. "Not even running. Walking."

"But up here!" the boy cried. "Way up here!"

"He do it every year," Sam said. "Once. Ash and Boon say he comes up here to run the other little bears away. Tell them to get to hell out of here and stay out until the hunters are gone. Maybe." The boy no longer heard anything at all, yet still Sam's head continued to turn gradually and steadily until the back of it was toward him. Then it turned back and looked down at him—the same face, grave, familiar, expressionless until it smiled, the same old man's eyes from which as he watched there faded slowly a quality darkly and fiercely lambent, passionate and proud. "He don't care no more for bears than he does for dogs or men neither. He come to see who's here, who's new in camp this year, whether he can shoot or not, can stay or not. Whether we got the dog yet that can bay and hold him until a man gets there with a gun. Because he's the head bear. He's the man." It faded, was gone; again they were the eyes as he had known them all his life. "He'll let them follow him to the river. Then he'll send them home. We might as well go too; see how they look when they get back to camp."

The dogs were there first, ten of them huddled back under the kitchen, himself and Sam squatting to peer back into the obscurity where they crouched, quiet, the eyes rolling and luminous, vanishing, and no sound, only that effluvium which the boy could not quite place yet, of something more than dog, stronger than dog and not just animal, just beast even. Because there had been nothing in front of the abject and painful yapping except the solitude, the wilderness, so that when the eleventh hound got back about mid-afternoon and he and Tennie's Jim held the passive and still trembling bitch while Sam daubed her tattered ear and raked shoulder with turpentine and axle-grease, it was still no living creature but only the wilderness which, leaning for a moment, had patted lightly once her temerity. "Just like a man," Sam said. "Just like folks. Put off as long as she could having to be brave, knowing all the time that sooner or later she would have to be brave once so she could keep on calling herself a dog, and knowing beforehand what was going to happen when she done it."

He did not know just when Sam left. He only knew that he was gone. For the next three mornings he rose and ate breakfast and Sam was not waiting for him. He went to his stand alone; he found it without help now and stood on it as Sam had taught him. On the third morning he heard the dogs again, running strong and free on a true scent again, and he readied the gun as he had learned to do and heard the hunt sweep past on since he was not ready yet, had not deserved other yet in just one short period of two weeks as compared to all the long life which he had already dedicated to the wilderness with patience and humility; he heard the shot again, one shot, the single clapping report of Walter Ewell's rifle. By now he could not only find his stand and then return to camp without guidance, by using the compass his cousin had given him he reached Walter waiting beside the buck and the moiling of dogs over the cast entrails before any of the others except Major de Spain and Tennie's Jim on the horses, even before Uncle Ash arrived with the one-eyed wagon-mule which did not mind the smell of blood or even, so they said, of bear.

It was not Uncle Ash on the mule. It was Sam, returned. And Sam was waiting when he finished his dinner and, himself on the one-eyed mule and Sam on the other one of the wagon team, they rode for more than three hours through the rapid shortening sunless afternoon, following no path, no trail even that he could discern, into a section of country he had never seen before. Then he understood why Sam had made him ride the one-eyed mule which would not spook at the smell of blood, of wild animals. The other one, the sound one, stopped short and tried to whirl and bolt even as Sam got down, jerking and wrenching at the rein while Sam held it, coaxing it forward with his voice since he did not dare risk hitching it, drawing it forward while the boy dismounted from the marred one which would stand. Then, standing beside Sam in the thick great gloom of ancient woods and the winter's dying afternoon, he looked quietly down at the rotted log scored and gutted with claw-marks and, in the wet earth beside it, the print of the enormous warped two-toed foot. Now he knew what he had heard in the hounds' voices in the woods that morning and what he had smelled when he peered under the kitchen where they huddled. It was in him too, a little different because they were brute beasts and he was not, but only a little different—an eagerness, passive; an abjectness, a sense of his own fragility and impotence against the timeless woods, yet without doubt or dread; a flavor like brass in the sudden run of saliva in his mouth, a hard sharp constriction either in his brain or his stomach, he could not tell which and it did not matter; he knew only that for the first time he realised that the bear which had run in his listening and loomed in his dreams since before he could remember and which therefore must have existed in the listening and the dreams of his cousin and Major de Spain and even old General Compson before they began to remember in their turn, was a mortal animal and that they had departed for the camp each November with no actual intention of slaying it, not because it could not be slain but because so far they had no actual hope of being able to.

"It will be tomorrow," he said.

"You mean we will try tomorrow," Sam said. "We ain't got the dog yet."

"We've got eleven," he said. "They ran him Monday."

"And you heard them," Sam said. "Saw them too. We ain't got the dog yet. It won't take but one. But he ain't there. Maybe he ain't nowhere. The only other way will be for him to run by accident over somebody that had a gun and knowed how to shoot it."

"That wouldn't be me," the boy said. "It would be Walter or Major or——"

"It might," Sam said. "You watch close tomorrow. Because he's smart. That's how come he has lived this long. If he gets hemmed up and has got to pick out somebody to run over, he will pick out you."

"How?" he said. "How will he know. . . ." He ceased. "You mean he already knows me, that I ain't never been to the big bottom before, ain't had time to find out yet whether I . . ." He ceased again, staring at Sam; he said humbly, not even amazed: "It was me he was watching. I don't reckon he did need to come but once."

"You watch tomorrow," Sam said. "I reckon we better start back. It'll be long after dark now before we get to camp."

The next morning they started three hours earlier than they had ever done. Even Uncle Ash went, the cook, who called himself by profession a camp cook and who did little else save cook for Major de Spain's hunting and camping parties, yet who had been marked by the wilderness from simple juxtaposition to it until he responded as they all did, even the boy who until two weeks ago had never even seen the wilderness, to a hound's ripped ear and shoulder and the print of a crooked foot in a patch of wet earth. They rode. It was too far to walk: the boy and Sam and Uncle Ash in the wagon with the dogs, his cousin and Major de Spain and General Compson and Boon and Walter and Ten-

nie's Jim riding double on the horses; again the first gray
light found him, as on that first morning two weeks ago, on
the stand where Sam had placed and left him. With the gun
which was too big for him, the breechloader which did not
even belong to him but to Major de Spain and which he had
fired only once, at a stump on the first day to learn the
recoil and how to reload it with the paper shells, he stood
against a big gum tree beside a little bayou whose black still
water crept without motion out of a cane-brake, across a
small clearing and into the cane again, where, invisible, a
bird, the big woodpecker called Lord-to-God by Negroes,
clattered at a dead trunk. It was a stand like any other stand,
dissimilar only in incidentals to the one where he had stood
each morning for two weeks; a territory new to him yet no
less familiar than that other one which after two weeks he
had come to believe he knew a little—the same solitude, the
same loneliness through which frail and timorous man had
merely passed without altering it, leaving no mark nor scar,
which looked exactly as it must have looked when the first
ancestor of Sam Father's Chickasaw predecessors crept into
it and looked about him, club or stone axe or bone arrow
drawn and ready, different only because, squatting at the
edge of the kitchen, he had smelled the dogs huddled and
cringing beneath it and saw the raked ear and side of the
bitch that, as Sam had said, had to be brave once in order to
keep on calling herself a dog, and saw yesterday in the earth
beside the gutted log, the print of the living foot. He heard
no dogs at all. He never did certainly hear them. He only
heard the drumming of the woodpecker stop short off, and

knew that the bear was looking at him. He never saw it. He did not know whether it was facing him from the cane or behind him. He did not move, holding the useless gun which he knew now he would never fire at it, now or ever, tasting in his saliva that taint of brass which he had smelled in the huddled dogs when he peered under the kitchen.

Then it was gone. As abruptly as it had stopped, the woodpecker's dry hammering set up again, and after a while he believed he even heard the dogs—a murmur, scarce a sound even, which he had probably been hearing for a time, perhaps a minute or two, before he remarked it, drifting into hearing and then out again, dying away. They came nowhere near him. If it was dogs he heard, he could not have sworn to it; if it was a bear they ran, it was another bear. It was Sam himself who emerged from the cane and crossed the bayou, the injured bitch following at heel as a bird dog is taught to walk. She came and crouched against his leg, trembling. "I didn't see him," he said. "I didn't, Sam."

"I know it," Sam said. "He done the looking. You didn't hear him neither, did you?"

"No," the boy said. "I——"

"He's smart," Sam said. "Too smart." Again the boy saw in his eyes that quality of dark and brooding lambency as Sam looked down at the bitch trembling faintly and steadily against the boy's leg. From her raked shoulder a few drops of fresh blood clung like bright berries. "Too big. We ain't got the dog yet. But maybe some day."

Because there would be a next time, after and after. He

was only ten. It seemed to him that he could see them, the two of them, shadowy in the limbo from which time emerged and became time: the old bear absolved of mortality and himself who shared a little of it. Because he recognised now what he had smelled in the huddled dogs and tasted in his own saliva, recognised fear as a boy, a youth, recognises the existence of love and passion and experience which is his heritage but not yet his patrimony, from entering by chance the presence or perhaps even merely the bedroom of a woman who has loved and been loved by many men. *So I will have to see him*, he thought, without dread or even hope. *I will have to look at him*. So it was in June of the next summer. They were at the camp again, celebrating Major de Spain's and General Compson's birthdays. Although the one had been born in September and the other in the depth of winter and almost thirty years earlier, each June the two of them and McCaslin and Boon and Walter Ewell (and the boy too from now on) spent two weeks at the camp, fishing and shooting squirrels and turkey and running coons and wildcats with the dogs at night. That is, Boon and the Negroes (and the boy too now) fished and shot squirrels and ran the coons and cats, because the proven hunters, not only Major de Spain and old General Compson (who spent those two weeks sitting in a rocking chair before a tremendous iron pot of Brunswick stew, stirring and tasting, with Uncle Ash to quarrel with about how he was making it and Tennie's Jim to pour whisky into the tin dipper from which he drank it) but even McCaslin and Walter Ewell who were still young enough, scorned such other than shooting the wild gobblers with pistols for wagers or to test their marksmanship.

That is, his cousin McCaslin and the others thought he was hunting squirrels. Until the third evening he believed that Sam Fathers thought so too. Each morning he would leave the camp right after breakfast. He had his own gun now, a new breech-loader, a Christmas gift; he would own and shoot it for almost seventy years, through two new pairs of barrels and locks and one new stock, until all that remained of the original gun was the silver-inlaid trigger-guard with his and McCaslin's engraved names and the date in 1878. He found the tree beside the little bayou where he had stood that morning. Using the compass he ranged from that point; he was teaching himself to be better than a fair woodsman without even knowing he was doing it. On the third day he even found the gutted log where he had first seen the print. It was almost completely crumbled now, healing with unbelievable speed, a passionate and almost visible relinquishment, back into the earth from which the tree had grown. He ranged the summer woods now, green with gloom, if anything actually dimmer than they had been in November's gray dissolution, where even at noon the sun fell only in windless dappling upon the earth which never completely dried and which crawled with snakes—moccasins and watersnakes and rattlers, themselves the color of the dappled gloom so that he would not always see them until they moved; returning to camp later and later and later, first day, second day, passing in the twilight of the third evening the little log pen enclosing the log barn where Sam was putting up the stock for the night. "You ain't looked right yet," Sam said.

He stopped. For a moment he didn't answer. Then he said peacefully, in a peaceful rushing burst, as when a boy's miniature dam in a little brook gives way: "All right. Yes. But how? I went to the bayou. I even found that log again. I——"

"I reckon that was all right. Likely he's been watching you. You never saw his foot?"

"I . . ." the boy said. "I didn't . . . I never thought . . ."

"It's the gun," Sam said. He stood beside the fence, motionless, the old man, son of a Negro slave and a Chickasaw chief, in the battered and faded overalls and the frayed five-cent straw hat which had been the badge of the Negro's slavery and was now the regalia of his freedom. The camp —the clearing, the house, the barn and its tiny lot with which Major de Spain in his turn had scratched punily and evanescently at the wilderness—faded in the dusk, back into the immemorial darkness of the woods. *The gun*, the boy thought. *The gun*. "You will have to choose," Sam said.

He left the next morning before light, without breakfast, long before Uncle Ash would wake in his quilts on the kitchen floor and start the fire. He had only the compass and a stick for the snakes. He could go almost a mile before he would need to see the compass. He sat on a log, the invisible compass in his hand, while the secret night-sounds which had ceased at his movements, scurried again and then fell still for good and the owls ceased and gave over to the waking day birds and there was light in the gray wet woods and he could see the compass. He went fast yet still quietly, becoming steadily better and better as a woodsman without yet having time to realise it; he jumped a doe and a fawn, walked them out of the bed, close enough to see them—the crash of undergrowth, the white scut, the fawn scudding along behind her, faster than he had known it could have run. He was hunting right, upwind, as Sam had taught him, but that didn't matter now. He had left the gun; by his own will and relinquishment he had accepted not a gambit, not a choice, but a condition in which not only the bear's heretofore inviolable anonymity but all the ancient rules and balances of hunter and hunted had been abrogated. He would not even be afraid, not even in the moment when the fear would take him completely: blood, skin, bowels, bones, memory from the long time before it even became his memory—all save that thin clear quenchless lucidity which alone differed him from this bear and from all the other bears and bucks he would follow during almost seventy years, to which Sam had said: "Be scared. You can't help that. But don't be afraid. Ain't nothing in the woods going to hurt you if you don't corner it or it don't smell that you are afraid. A bear or a deer has got to be scared of a coward the same as a brave man has got to be."

By noon he was far beyond the crossing on the little bayou, farther into the new and alien country than he had ever been, travelling now not only by the compass but by the old, heavy, biscuit-thick silver watch which had been his father's. He had left the camp nine hours ago; nine hours from now, dark would already have been an hour old. He stopped, for the first time since he had risen from the log when he could see the compass face at last, and looked about, mopping his sweating face on his sleeve. He had already relinquished, of his will, because of his need, in humility and peace and without regret, yet apparently that had not been enough, the leaving of the gun was not enough. He stood for a moment—a child, alien and lost in the green and soaring gloom of the markless wilderness. Then he relinquished completely to it. It was the watch and the compass. He was still tainted. He removed the linked chain of the one and the looped thong of the other from his overalls and hung them on a bush and leaned the stick beside them and entered it.

When he realised he was lost, he did as Sam had coached and drilled him: made a cast to cross his backtrack. He had not been going very fast for the last two or three hours, and he had gone even less fast since he left the compass and watch on the bush. So he went slower still now, since the tree could not be very far; in fact, he found it before he really expected to and turned and went to it. But there was no bush beneath it, no compass nor watch, so he did next as Sam had coached and drilled him: made this next circle in the opposite direction and much larger, so that the pattern of the two of them would bisect his track somewhere, but crossing no trace nor mark anywhere of his feet or any feet, and now he was going faster though still not panicked, his heart beating a little more rapidly but strong and steady enough, and this time it was not even the tree because there was a down log beside it which he had never seen before

and beyond the log a little swamp, a seepage of moisture
somewhere between earth and water, and he did what Sam
had coached and drilled him as the next and the last, seeing as
he sat down on the log the crooked print, the warped in-
dentation in the wet ground which while he looked at it
continued to fill with water until it was level full and the
water began to overflow and the sides of the print began to
dissolve away. Even as he looked up he saw the next one,
and, moving, the one beyond it; moving, not hurrying, running, but merely keeping pace with them as they appeared
before him as though they were being shaped out of thin
air just one constant pace short of where he would lose
them forever and be lost forever himself, tireless, eager,
without doubt or dread, panting a little above the strong
rapid little hammer of his heart, emerging suddenly into a
little glade and the wilderness coalesced. It rushed, soundless, and solidified—the tree, the bush, the compass and the
watch glinting where a ray of sunlight touched them. Then
he saw the bear. It did not emerge, appear: it was just there,
immobile, fixed in the green and windless noon's hot dappling, not as big as he had dreamed it but as big as he had
expected, bigger, dimensionless against the dappled obscurity, looking at him. Then it moved. It crossed the glade
without haste, walking for an instant into the sun's full glare
and out of it, and stopped again and looked back at him
across one shoulder. Then it was gone. It didn't walk into
the woods. It faded, sank back into the wilderness without
motion as he had watched a fish, a huge old bass, sink back

into the dark depths of its pool and vanish without even any
movement of its fins.

2. So he should have hated and feared Lion. He
was thirteen then. He had killed his buck and Sam Fathers
had marked his face with the hot blood, and in the next
November he killed a bear. But before that accolade he
had become as competent in the woods as many grown
men with the same experience. By now he was a better
woodsman than most grown men with more. There was
no territory within twenty-five miles of the camp that he
did not know—bayou, ridge, landmark trees and path; he
could have led anyone direct to any spot in it and brought
him back. He knew game trails that even Sam Fathers had
never seen; in the third fall he found a buck's bedding-
place by himself and unbeknown to his cousin he borrowed Walter Ewell's rifle and lay in wait for the buck at
dawn and killed it when it walked back to the bed as Sam
had told him how the old Chickasaw fathers did.

By now he knew the old bear's footprint better than he
did his own, and not only the crooked one. He could see
any one of the three sound prints and distinguish it at once
from any other, and not only because of its size. There were
other bears within that fifty miles which left tracks almost
as large, or at least so near that the one would have appeared larger only by juxtaposition. It was more than that.
If Sam Fathers had been his mentor and the backyard
rabbits and squirrels his kindergarten, then the wilderness

the old bear ran was his college and the old male bear itself, so long unwifed and childless as to have become its own ungendered progenitor, was his alma mater.

He could find the crooked print now whenever he wished, ten miles or five miles or sometimes closer than that, to the camp. Twice while on stand during the next three years he heard the dogs strike its trail and once even jump it by chance, the voices high, abject, almost human in their hysteria. Once, still-hunting with Walter Ewell's rifle, he saw it cross a long corridor of down timber where a tornado had passed. It rushed through rather than across the tangle of trunks and branches as a locomotive would, faster than he had ever believed it could have moved, almost as fast as a deer even because the deer would have spent most of that distance in the air; he realised then why it would take a dog not only of abnormal courage but size and speed too ever to bring it to bay. He had a little dog at home, a mongrel, of the sort called fyce by Negroes, a ratter, itself not much bigger than a rat and possessing that sort of courage which had long since stopped being bravery and had become foolhardiness. He brought it with him one June and, timing them as if they were meeting an appointment with another human being, himself carrying the fyce with a sack over its head and Sam Fathers with a brace of the hounds on a rope leash, they lay downwind of the trail and actually ambushed the bear. They were so close that it turned at bay although he realised later this might have been from surprise and amazement at the shrill and frantic uproar of the fyce. It turned at bay against the trunk of a big cypress, on its hind feet; it seemed to the boy that it would never stop rising, taller and taller, and even the two hounds seemed to have taken a kind of desperate and despairing courage from the fyce. Then he realised that the fyce was actually not going to stop. He flung the gun down and ran. When he overtook and grasped the shrill, frantically pinwheeling little dog, it seemed to him that he was directly under the bear. He could smell it, strong and hot and rank. Sprawling, he looked up where it loomed and towered over him like a thunderclap. It was quite familiar, until he remembered: this was the way he had used to dream about it.

Then it was gone. He didn't see it go. He knelt, holding the frantic fyce with both hands, hearing the abased wailing of the two hounds drawing further and further away, until Sam came up, carrying the gun. He laid it quietly down beside the boy and stood looking down at him. "You've done seed him twice now, with a gun in your hands," he said. "This time you couldn't have missed him."

The boy rose. He still held the fyce. Even in his arms it continued to yap frantically, surging and straining toward the fading sound of the hounds like a collection of live-wire springs. The boy was panting a little. "Neither could you," he said. "You had the gun. Why didn't you shoot him?"

Sam didn't seem to have heard. He put out his hand and touched the little dog in the boy's arms which still yapped and strained even though the two hounds were out of hearing now. "He's done gone," Sam said. "You can slack off and rest now, until next time." He stroked the little dog until it began to grow quiet under his hand. "You's almost the one we wants," he said. "You just ain't big enough. We ain't got that one yet. He will need to be just a little bigger than smart, and a little braver than either." He withdrew his hand from the fyce's head and stood looking into the woods where the bear and the hounds had vanished. "Somebody is going to, some day."

"I know it," the boy said. "That's why it must be one of us. So it won't be until the last day. When even he don't want it to last any longer."

So he should have hated and feared Lion. It was in the fourth summer, the fourth time he had made one in the celebration of Major de Spain's and General Compson's birthday. In the early spring Major de Spain's mare had foaled a horse colt. One evening when Sam brought the horses and mules up to stable them for the night, the colt was missing and it was all he could do to get the frantic mare into the lot. He had thought at first to let the mare lead him back to where she had become separated from the foal. But she would not do it. She would not even feint toward any particular part of the woods or even in any particular direction. She merely ran, as if she couldn't see, still frantic with terror. She whirled and ran at Sam once, as if to attack him in some ultimate desperation, as if she could not for the moment realise that he was a man and a long-familiar one. He got her into the lot at last. It was too dark by that time to back-track her, to unravel the erratic course she had doubtless pursued.

He came to the house and told Major de Spain. It was an animal, of course, a big one, and the colt was dead now, wherever it was. They all knew that. "It's a panther," General Compson said at once. "The same one. That doe and fawn last March." Sam had sent Major de Spain word of it when Boon Hogganbeck came to the camp on a routine visit to see how the stock had wintered—the doe's throat torn out, and the beast had run down the helpless fawn and killed it too.

"Sam never did say that was a panther," Major de Spain said. Sam said nothing now, standing behind Major de Spain where they sat at supper, inscrutable, as if he were just waiting for them to stop talking so he could go home. He didn't even seem to be looking at anything. "A panther might jump a doe, and he wouldn't have much trouble catching the fawn afterward. But no panther would have jumped that colt with the dam right there with it. It was Old Ben," Major de Spain said. "I'm disappointed in him. He has broken the rules. I didn't think he would have done that. He has killed mine and McCaslin's dogs, but that was all right. We gambled the dogs against him; we gave each other warning. But now he has come into my house and destroyed my property, out of season too. He broke the rules. It was Old Ben, Sam." Still Sam said nothing, standing there until Major de Spain should stop talking. "We'll back-track her tomorrow and see," Major de Spain said.

Sam departed. He would not live in the camp; he had built himself a little hut something like Joe Baker's, only stouter, tighter, on the bayou a quarter-mile away, and a stout log crib where he stored a little corn for the shoat he raised each year. The next morning he was waiting when they waked. He had already found the colt. They did not even wait for breakfast. It was not far, not five hundred yards from the stable—the three-months' colt lying on its side, its throat torn out and the entrails and one ham partly eaten. It lay not as if it had been dropped but as if it had been struck and hurled, and no cat-mark, no claw-mark where a panther would have gripped it while finding its throat. They read the tracks where the frantic mare had circled and at last rushed in with that same ultimate desperation with which she had whirled on Sam Fathers yesterday evening, and the long tracks of dead and terrified running and those of the beast which had not even rushed at her when she advanced but had merely walked three or four paces toward her until she broke, and General Compson said, "Good God, what a wolf!"

Still Sam said nothing. The boy watched him while the men knelt, measuring the tracks. There was something in Sam's face now. It was neither exultation nor joy nor hope. Later, a man, the boy realised what it had been, and that Sam had known all the time what had made the tracks and what had torn the throat out of the doe in the spring and killed the fawn. It had been foreknowledge in Sam's face that morning. *And he was glad*, he told himself. *He was old. He had no children, no people, none of his blood anywhere above earth that he would ever meet again. And even if he were to, he could not have touched it, spoken to it, because for seventy years now he had had to be a Negro. It was almost over now and he was glad.*

They returned to camp and had breakfast and came back with guns and the hounds. Afterward the boy realised that they also should have known then what killed the colt as well as Sam Fathers did. But that was neither the first nor the last time he had seen men rationalise from and even act upon their misconceptions. After Boon, standing astride the colt, had whipped the dogs away from it with his belt, they snuffed at the tracks. One of them, a young dog hound without judgment yet, bayed once, and they ran for a few feet on what seemed to be a trail. Then they stopped, looking back at the men, eager enough, not baffled, merely questioning, as if they were asking "Now what?" Then they rushed back to the colt, where Boon, still astride it, slashed at them with the belt.

"I never knew a trail to get cold that quick," General Compson said.

"Maybe a single wolf big enough to kill a colt with the dam right there beside it don't leave scent," Major de Spain said.

"Maybe it was a hant," Walter Ewell said. He looked at Tennie's Jim. "Hah, Jim?"

Because the hounds would not run it, Major de Spain had Sam hunt out and find the tracks a hundred yards farther on and they put the dogs on it again and again the young one bayed and not one of them realised then that the hound was not baying like a dog striking game but was merely bellowing like a country dog whose yard has been invaded. General Compson spoke to the boy and Boon and Tennie's Jim: to the squirrel hunters. "You boys keep the dogs with you this morning. He's probably hanging around somewhere, waiting to get his breakfast off the colt. You might strike him."

But they did not. The boy remembered how Sam stood watching them as they went into the woods with the leashed hounds—the Indian face in which he had never seen anything until it smiled, except that faint arching of the nostrils on that first morning when the hounds had found Old Ben. They took the hounds with them on the next day, though when they reached the place where they hoped to strike a fresh trail, the carcass of the colt was gone.

Then on the third morning Sam was waiting again, this time until they had finished breakfast. He said, "Come." He led them to his house, his little hut, to the corn-crib beyond it. He had removed the corn and had made a deadfall of the door, baiting it with the colt's carcass; peering between the logs, they saw an animal almost the color of a gun or pistol barrel, what little time they had to examine its color or shape. It was not crouched nor even standing. It was in motion, in the air, coming toward them—a heavy body crashing with tremendous force against the door so that the thick door jumped and clattered in its frame, the animal, whatever it was, hurling itself against the door again seemingly before it could have touched the floor and got a new purchase to spring from. "Come away," Sam said, "fore he break his neck." Even when they retreated the heavy and measured crashes continued, the stout door jumping and clattering each time, and still no sound from the beast itself—no snarl, no cry.

"What in hell's name is it?" Major de Spain said.

"It's a dog," Sam said, his nostrils arching and collapsing faintly and steadily and that faint, fierce milkiness in his eyes again as on that first morning when the hounds had struck the old bear. "It's the dog."

"*The* dog?" Major de Spain said.

"That's gonter hold Old Ben."

"Dog the devil," Major de Spain said. "I'd rather have Old Ben himself in my pack than that brute. Shoot him."

"No," Sam said.

"You'll never tame him. How do you ever expect to make an animal like that afraid of you?"

"I don't want him tame," Sam said; again the boy watched his nostrils and the fierce milky light in his eyes. "But I almost rather he be tame than scared, of me or any man or any thing. But he won't be neither, of nothing."

"Then what are you going to do with it?"

"You can watch," Sam said.

Each morning through the second week they would go to Sam's crib. He had removed a few shingles from the roof and had put a rope on the colt's carcass and had drawn it out when the trap fell. Each morning they would watch him lower a pail of water into the crib while the dog hurled itself tirelessly against the door and dropped back and leaped again. It never made any sound and there was nothing frenzied in the act but only a cold and grim indomitable determination. Toward the end of the week it stopped jumping at the door. Yet it had not weakened appreciably and it was not as if it had rationalised the fact that the door was not going to give. It was as if for that time it simply disdained to jump any longer. It was not down. None of them had ever seen it down. It stood, and they could see it now—part mastiff, something of Airedale and something of a dozen other strains probably, better than thirty inches at the shoulders and weighing as they guessed almost ninety pounds, with cold yellow eyes and a tremendous chest and over all that strange color like a blued gun-barrel.

Then the two weeks were up. They prepared to break camp. The boy begged to remain and his cousin let him. He moved into the little hut with Sam Fathers. Each morning he watched Sam lower the pail of water into the crib. By the end of that week the dog was down. It would rise and half stagger, half crawl to the water and drink and collapse again. One morning it could not even reach the water, could not raise its forequarters even from the floor. Sam took a short stick and prepared to enter the crib. "Wait," the boy said. "Let me get the gun——"

"No," Sam said. "He can't move now." Nor could it. It lay on its side while Sam touched it, its head and the gaunted body, the dog lying motionless, the yellow eyes open. They were not fierce and there was nothing of petty malevolence in them, but a cold and almost impersonal malignance like some natural force. It was not even looking at Sam nor at the boy peering at it between the logs.

Sam began to feed it again. The first time he had to

raise its head so it could lap the broth. That night he left a bowl of broth containing lumps of meat where the dog could reach it. The next morning the bowl was empty and the dog was lying on its belly, its head up, the cold yellow eyes watching the door as Sam entered, no change whatever in the cold yellow eyes and still no sound from it even when it sprang, its aim and co-ordination still bad from weakness so that Sam had time to strike it down with the stick and leap from the crib and slam the door as the dog, still without having had time to get its feet under it to jump again seemingly, hurled itself against the door as if the two weeks of starving had never been.

At noon that day someone came whooping through the woods from the direction of the camp. It was Boon. He came and looked for a while between the logs, at the tremendous dog lying again on its belly, its head up, the yellow eyes blinking sleepily at nothing: the indomitable and unbroken spirit. "What we beter do," Boon said, "is to let that son of a bitch go and catch Old Ben and run him on the dog." He turned to the boy his weather-reddened and beetling face. "Get your traps together. Cass says for you to come on home. You been in here fooling with that horse-eating varmint long enough."

Boon had a borrowed mule at the camp; the buggy was waiting at the edge of the bottom. He was at home that night. He told McCaslin about it. "Sam's going to starve him again until he can go in and touch him. Then he will feed him again. Then he will starve him again, if he has to."

"But why?" McCaslin said. "What for? Even Sam will never tame that brute."

"We don't want him tame. We want him like he is. We just want him to find out at last that the only way he can get out of that crib and stay out of it is to do what Sam or somebody tells him to do. He's the dog that's going to stop Old Ben and hold him. We've already named him. His name is Lion."

Then November came at last. They returned to the camp. With General Compson and Major de Spain and his cousin and Walter and Boon he stood in the yard among the guns and bedding and boxes of food and watched Sam Fathers and Lion come up the lane from the lot—the Indian, the old man in battered overalls and rubber boots and a worn sheepskin coat and a hat which had belonged to the boy's father; the tremendous dog pacing gravely beside him. The hounds rushed out to meet them and stopped, except the young one which still had but little of judgment. It ran up to Lion, fawning. Lion didn't snap at it. He didn't even pause. He struck it rolling and yelping for five or six feet with a blow of one paw as a bear would have done and came on into the yard and stood, blinking sleepily at nothing, looking at no one, while Boon said, "Jesus. Jesus.—Will he let me touch him?"

"You can touch him," Sam said. "He don't care. He don't care about nothing or nobody."

The boy watched that too. He watched it for the next two years from that moment when Boon touched Lion's head and then knelt beside him, feeling the bones and

muscles, the power. It was as if Lion were a woman—or
perhaps Boon was the woman. That was more like it—the
big, grave, sleepy-seeming dog which, as Sam Fathers said,
cared about no man and no thing; and the violent, insensi-
tive, hard-faced man with his touch of remote Indian blood
and the mind almost of a child. He watched Boon take
over Lion's feeding from Sam and Uncle Ash both. He
would see Boon squatting in the cold rain beside the
kitchen while Lion ate. Because Lion neither slept nor ate
with the other dogs though none of them knew where he
did sleep until in the second November, thinking until then
that Lion slept in his kennel beside Sam Fathers' hut, when
the boy's cousin McCaslin said something about it to Sam
by sheer chance and Sam told him. And that night the boy
and Major de Spain and McCaslin with a lamp entered the
back room where Boon slept—the little, tight, airless room
rank with the smell of Boon's unwashed body and his wet
hunting-clothes—where Boon, snoring on his back, choked
and waked and Lion raised his head beside him and looked
back from his cold, slumbrous yellow eyes.

"Damn it, Boon," McCaslin said. "Get that dog out of
here. He's got to run Old Ben tomorrow morning. How in
hell do you expect him to smell anything fainter than a
skunk after breathing you all night?"

"The way I smell ain't hurt my nose none that I ever
noticed," Boon said.

"It wouldn't matter if it had," Major de Spain said.
"We're not depending on you to trail a bear. Put him outside. Put him under the house with the other dogs."

Boon began to get up. "He'll kill the first one that happens to yawn or sneeze in his face or touches him."

"I reckon not," Major de Spain said. "None of them are going to risk yawning in his face or touching him either, even asleep. Put him outside. I want his nose right tomorrow. Old Ben fooled him last year. I don't think he will do it again."

Boon put on his shoes without lacing them; in his long soiled underwear, his hair still tousled from sleep, he and Lion went out. The others returned to the front room and the poker game where McCaslin's and Major de Spain's hands waited for them on the table. After a while McCaslin said, "Do you want me to go back and look again?"

"No," Major de Spain said. "I call," he said to Walter Ewell. He spoke to McCaslin again. "If you do, don't tell me. I am beginning to see the first sign of my increasing age: I don't like to know that my orders have been disobeyed, even when I knew when I gave them that they would be.—A small pair," he said to Walter Ewell.

"How small?" Walter said.

"Very small," Major de Spain said.

And the boy, lying beneath his piled quilts and blankets waiting for sleep, knew likewise that Lion was already back in Boon's bed, for the rest of that night and the next one and during all the nights of the next November and the next one. He thought then: *I wonder what Sam thinks. He could have Lion with him, even if Boon is a white man. He could ask Major or McCaslin either. And more than that. It was Sam's hand that touched Lion first and Lion knows it.* Then he became a man and he knew that too. It had been all right. That was the way it should have been. Sam was the chief, the prince; Boon, the plebeian, was his huntsman. Boon should have nursed the dogs.

On the first morning that Lion led the pack after Old Ben, seven strangers appeared in the camp. They were swampers: gaunt, malaria-ridden men appearing from no-where, who ran trap-lines for coons or perhaps farmed little patches of cotton and corn along the edge of the bottom, in clothes but little better than Sam Fathers' and nowhere near as good as Tennie's Jim's, with worn shotguns and rifles, already squatting patiently in the cold drizzle in the side yard when day broke. They had a spokesman; after-ward Sam Fathers told Major de Spain how all during the past summer and fall they had drifted into the camp singly or in pairs and threes, to look quietly at Lion for a while and then go away: "Mawnin, Major. We heerd you was aimin to put that ere blue dawg on that old two-toed bear this mawnin. We figgered we'd come up and watch, it you don't mind. We won't do no shooting, lessen he runs over us."

"You are welcome," Major de Spain said. "You are wel-come to shoot. He's more your bear than ours."

"I reckon that ain't no lie. I done fed him enough cawn to have a sheer in him. Not to mention a shoat three years ago."

"I reckon I got a sheer too," another said. "Only it ain't in the bear." Major de Spain looked at him. He was chew-ing tobacco. He spat. "Hit was a heifer calf. Nice un too.

Last year. When I finally found her, I reckon she looked about like that colt of yourn looked last June."

"Oh," Major de Spain said. "Be welcome. If you see game in front of my dogs, shoot it."

Nobody shot Old Ben that day. No man saw him. The dogs jumped him within a hundred yards of the glade where the boy had seen him that day in the summer of his eleventh year. The boy was less than a quarter-mile away. He heard the jump but he could distinguish no voice among the dogs that he did not know and therefore would be Lion's, and he thought, believed, that Lion was not among them. Even the fact that they were going much faster than he had ever heard them run behind Old Ben before and that the high thin note of hysteria was missing now from their voices was not enough to disabuse him. He didn't comprehend until that night, when Sam told him that Lion would never cry on a trail. "He gonter growl when he catches Old Ben's throat," Sam said. "But he ain't gonter never holler, no more than he ever done when he was jumping at that two-inch door. It's that blue dog in him. What you call it?"

"Airedale," the boy said.

Lion was there; the jump was just too close to the river. When Boon returned with Lion about eleven that night, he swore that Lion had stopped Old Ben once but that the hounds would not go in and Old Ben broke away and took to the river and swam for miles down it and he and Lion went down one bank for about ten miles and crossed and came up the other but it had begun to get dark before they

struck any trail where Old Ben had come up out of the
water, unless he was still in the water when he passed the
ford where they crossed. Then he fell to cursing the hounds
and ate the supper Uncle Ash had saved for him and went
off to bed and after a while the boy opened the door of the
little stale room thunderous with snoring and the great
grave dog raised its head from Boon's pillow and blinked
at him for a moment and lowered its head again.

When the next November came and the last day, the
day on which it was now becoming traditional to save for
Old Ben, there were more than a dozen strangers waiting.
They were not all swampers this time. Some of them were
townsmen, from other county seats like Jefferson, who had
heard about Lion and Old Ben and had come to watch the
great blue dog keep his yearly rendezvous with the old
two-toed bear. Some of them didn't even have guns and the
hunting-clothes and boots they wore had been on a store
shelf yesterday.

This time Lion jumped Old Ben more than five miles
from the river and bayed and held him and this time the
hounds went in, in a sort of desperate emulation. The boy
heard them; he was that near. He heard Boon whooping;
he heard the two shots when General Compson delivered
both barrels, one containing five buckshot, the other a
single ball, into the bear from as close as he could force his
almost unmanageable horse. He heard the dogs when the
bear broke free again. He was running now; panting,
stumbling, his lungs bursting, he reached the place where
General Compson had fired and where Old Ben had killed

two of the hounds. He saw the blood from General Compson's shots, but he could go no further. He stopped, leaning against a tree for his breathing to ease and his heart to slow, hearing the sound of the dogs as it faded on and died away.

In camp that night—they had as guests five of the still terrified strangers in new hunting coats and boots who had been lost all day until Sam Fathers went out and got them —he heard the rest of it: how Lion had stopped and held the bear again but only the one-eyed mule which did not mind the smell of wild blood would approach and Boon was riding the mule and Boon had never been known to hit anything. He shot at the bear five times with his pump gun, touching nothing, and Old Ben killed another hound and broke free once more and reached the river and was gone. Again Boon and Lion hunted as far down one bank as they dared. Too far; they crossed in the first of dusk and dark overtook them within a mile. And this time Lion found the broken trail, the blood perhaps, in the darkness where Old Ben had come up out of the water, but Boon had him on a rope, luckily, and he got down from the mule and fought Lion hand-to-hand until he got him back to camp. This time Boon didn't even curse. He stood in the door, muddy, spent, his huge gargoyle's face tragic and still amazed. "I missed him," he said. "I was in twenty-five feet of him and I missed him five times."

"But we have drawn blood," Major de Spain said. "General Compson drew blood. We have never done that before."

"But I missed him," Boon said. "I missed him five times. With Lion looking right at me."

"Never mind," Major de Spain said. "It was a damned fine race. And we drew blood. Next year we'll let General Compson or Walter ride Katie, and we'll get him."

Then McCaslin said, "Where is Lion, Boon?"

"I left him at Sam's," Boon said. He was already turning away. "I ain't fit to sleep with him."

So he should have hated and feared Lion. Yet he did not. It seemed to him that there was a fatality in it. It seemed to him that something, he didn't know what, was beginning; had already begun. It was like the last act on a set stage. It was the beginning of the end of something, he didn't know what except that he would not grieve. He would be humble and proud that he had been found worthy to be a part of it too or even just to see it too.

3. It was December. It was the coldest December he had ever remembered. They had been in camp four days over two weeks, waiting for the weather to soften so that Lion and Old Ben could run their yearly race. Then they would break camp and go home. Because of these unforeseen additional days which they had had to pass waiting on the weather, with nothing to do but play poker, the whisky had given out and he and Boon were being sent to Memphis with a suitcase and a note from Major de Spain to Mr. Semmes, the distiller, to get more. That is, Major de Spain and McCaslin were sending Boon to get

the whisky and sending him to see that Boon got back
with it or most of it or at least some of it.

Tennie's Jim waked him at three. He dressed rapidly,
shivering, not so much from the cold because a fresh fire
already boomed and roared on the hearth, but in that dead
winter hour when the blood and the heart are slow and
sleep is incomplete. He crossed the gap between house
and kitchen, the gap of iron earth beneath the brilliant and
rigid night where dawn would not begin for three hours
yet, tasting, tongue palate and to the very bottom of his
lungs the searing dark, and entered the kitchen, the lamp-
lit warmth where the stove glowed, fogging the windows,
and where Boon already sat at the table at breakfast,
hunched over his plate, almost in his plate, his working
jaws blue with stubble and his face innocent of water and
his coarse, horse-mane hair innocent of comb—the quarter
Indian, grandson of a Chickasaw squaw, who on occasion
resented with his hard and furious fists the intimation of
one single drop of alien blood and on others, usually after
whisky, affirmed with the same fists and the same fury
that his father had been the full-blood Chickasaw and even
a chief and that even his mother had been only half white.
He was four inches over six feet; he had the mind of a
child, the heart of a horse, and little hard shoe-button eyes
without depth or meanness or generosity or viciousness or
gentleness or anything else, in the ugliest face the boy had
ever seen. It looked like somebody had found a walnut a
little larger than a football and with a machinist's hammer
had shaped features into it and then painted it, mostly red;

not Indian red but a fine bright ruddy color which whisky might have had something to do with but which was mostly just happy and violent out-of-doors, the wrinkles in it not the residue of the forty years it had survived but from squinting into the sun or into the gloom of cane-brakes where game had run, baked into it by the camp fires before which he had lain trying to sleep on the cold November or December ground while waiting for daylight so he could rise and hunt again, as though time were merely something he walked through as he did through air, aging him no more than air did. He was brave, faithful, improvident and unreliable; he had neither profession, job nor trade and owned one vice and one virtue: whisky, and that absolute and unquestioning fidelity to Major de Spain and the boy's cousin McCaslin. "Sometimes I'd call them both virtues," Major de Spain said once. "Or both vices," McCaslin said.

He ate his breakfast, hearing the dogs under the kitchen, wakened by the smell of frying meat or perhaps by the feet overhead. He heard Lion once, short and peremptory, as the best hunter in any camp has only to speak once to all save the fools, and none other of Major de Spain's and McCaslin's dogs were Lion's equal in size and strength and perhaps even in courage, but they were not fools; Old Ben had killed the last fool among them last year.

Tennie's Jim came in as they finished. The wagon was outside. Ash decided he would drive them over to the log-line where they would flag the outbound log-train and let Tennie's Jim wash the dishes. The boy knew why. It would not be the first time he had listened to old Ash badgering Boon.

It was cold. The wagon wheels banged and clattered on the frozen ground; the sky was fixed and brilliant. He was not shivering, he was shaking, slow and steady and hard, the food he had just eaten still warm and solid inside him while his outside shook slow and steady around it as though his stomach floated loose. "They won't run this morning," he said. "No dog will have any nose today."

"Cep Lion," Ash said. "Lion don't need no nose. All he need is a bear." He had wrapped his feet in towsacks and he had a quilt from his pallet bed on the kitchen floor drawn over his head and wrapped around him until in the thin brilliant starlight he looked like nothing at all that the boy had ever seen before. "He run a bear through a thousand-acre ice-house. Catch him too. Them other dogs don't matter, because they ain't going to keep up with Lion nohow, long as he got a bear in front of him."

"What's wrong with the other dogs?" Boon said. "What the hell do you know about it anyway? This is the first time you've had your tail out of that kitchen since we got here except to chop a little wood."

"Ain't nothing wrong with them," Ash said. "And long as it's left up to them, ain't nothing going to be. I just wish I had knowed all my life how to take care of my health good as them hounds knows."

"Well, they ain't going to run this morning," Boon said. His voice was harsh and positive. "Major promised they wouldn't until me and Ike get back."

"Weather gonter break today. Gonter soft up. Rain by night." Then Ash laughed, chuckled, somewhere inside the quilt which concealed even his face. "Hum up here, mules!" he said, jerking the reins so that the mules leaped forward and snatched the lurching and banging wagon for several feet before they slowed again into their quick, short-paced, rapid plodding. "Sides, I like to know why Major need to wait on you. It's Lion he aiming to use. I ain't never heard tell of you bringing no bear nor no other kind of meat into this camp."

Now Boon's going to curse Ash or maybe even hit him, the boy thought. But Boon never did, never had; the boy knew he never would even though four years ago Boon had shot five times with a borrowed pistol at a Negro on the street in Jefferson, with the same result as when he had shot five times at Old Ben last fall. "By God," Boon said, "he ain't going to put Lion or no other dog on nothing until I get back tonight. Because he promised me. Whip up them mules and keep them whipped up. Do you want me to freeze to death?"

They reached the log-line and built a fire. After a while the log train came up out of the woods under the paling east and Boon flagged it. Then in the warm caboose the boy slept again while Boon and the conductor and brakeman talked about Lion and Old Ben as people later would talk about Sullivan and Kilrain and, later still, about Dempsey and Tunney. Dozing, swaying as the springless caboose lurched and clattered, he would hear them still talking, about the shoats and calves Old Ben had killed and the cribs he had rifled and the traps and deadfalls he had wrecked and the lead he probably carried under his hide— Old Ben, the two-toed bear in a land where bears with trap-ruined feet had been called Two-Toe or Three-Toe or Cripple-Foot for fifty years, only Old Ben was an extra bear (the head bear, General Compson called him) and so had earned a name such as a human man could have worn and not been sorry.

They reached Hoke's at sunup. They emerged from the warm caboose in their hunting clothes, the muddy boots and stained khaki and Boon's blue unshaven jowls. But that was all right. Hoke's was a sawmill and commissary and two stores and a loading-chute on a sidetrack from the main line, and all the men in it wore boots and khaki too. Presently the Memphis train came. Boon bought three packages of popcorn-and-molasses and a bottle of beer from the news butch and the boy went to sleep again to the sound of his chewing.

But in Memphis it was not all right. It was as if the high buildings and the hard pavements, the fine carriages and the horse cars and the men in starched collars and neckties made their boots and khaki look a little rougher and a little muddier and made Boon's beard look worse and more unshaven and his face look more and more like he should never have brought it out of the woods at all or at least out of reach of Major de Spain or McCaslin or someone who knew it and could have said, "Don't be afraid. He won't hurt you." He walked through the station, on the slick floor, his face moving as he worked the popcorn out of his teeth

with his tongue, his legs spraddled and stiff in the hips as
if he were walking on buttered glass, and that blue stubble
on his face like the filings from a new gun-barrel. They
passed the first saloon. Even through the closed doors the
boy could seem to smell the sawdust and the reek of old
drink. Boon began to cough. He coughed for something
less than a minute. "Damn this cold," he said. "I'd sure
like to know where I got it."

"Back there in the station," the boy said.

Boon had started to cough again. He stopped. He looked
at the boy. "What?" he said.

"You never had it when we left camp nor on the train
either." Boon looked at him, blinking. Then he stopped
blinking. He didn't cough again. He said quietly:

"Lend me a dollar. Come on. You've got it. If you ever
had one, you've still got it. I don't mean you are tight with
your money because you ain't. You just don't never seem
to ever think of nothing you want. When I was sixteen a
dollar bill melted off of me before I even had time to read
the name of the bank that issued it." He said quietly: "Let
me have a dollar, Ike."

"You promised Major. You promised McCaslin. Not till
we get back to camp."

"All right," Boon said in that quiet and patient voice.
"What can I do on just one dollar? You ain't going to lend
me another."

"You're damn right I ain't," the boy said, his voice quiet
too, cold with rage which was not at Boon, remembering:
Boon snoring in a hard chair in the kitchen so he could

watch the clock and wake him and McCaslin and drive
them the seventeen miles in to Jefferson to catch the train
to Memphis; the wild, never-bridled Texas paint pony
which he had persuaded McCaslin to let him buy and
which he and Boon had bought at auction for four dollars
and seventy-five cents and fetched home wired between two
gentle old mares with pieces of barbed wire and which had
never even seen shelled corn before and didn't even know
what it was unless the grains were bugs maybe and at last
(he was ten and Boon had been ten all his life) Boon said
the pony was gentled and with a towsack over its head and
four Negroes to hold it they backed it into an old two-
wheeled cart and hooked up the gear and he and Boon got
up and Boon said, "All right, boys. Let him go," and one
of the Negroes—it was Tennie's Jim—snatched the towsack off and leaped for his life and they lost the first wheel
against a post of the open gate only at that moment Boon
caught him by the scruff of the neck and flung him into the
roadside ditch so he only saw the rest of it in fragments:
the other wheel as it slammed through the side gate and
crossed the back yard and leaped up onto the gallery and
scraps of the cart here and there along the road and Boon
vanishing rapidly on his stomach in the leaping and spurt-
ing dust and still holding the reins until they broke too and
two days later they finally caught the pony seven miles
away still wearing the hames and the headstall of the
bridle around its neck like a duchess with two necklaces at
one time. He gave Boon the dollar.

"All right," Boon said. "Come on in out of the cold."

"I ain't cold," he said.

"You can have some lemonade."

"I don't want any lemonade."

The door closed behind him. The sun was well up now. It was a brilliant day, though Ash had said it would rain before night. Already it was warmer; they could run tomorrow. He felt the old lift of the heart, as pristine as ever, as on the first day; he would never lose it, no matter how old in hunting and pursuit: the best, the best of all breathing, the humility and the pride. He must stop thinking about it. Already it seemed to him that he was running, back to the station, to the tracks themselves: the first train going south; he must stop thinking about it. The street was busy. He wached the big Norman draft horses, the Percherons; the trim carriages from which the men in the fine overcoats and the ladies rosy in furs descended and entered the station. (They were still next door to it but one.) Twenty years ago his father had ridden into Memphis as a member of Colonel Sartoris' horse in Forrest's command, up Main street and (the tale told) into the lobby of the Gayoso Hotel where the Yankee officers sat in the leather chairs spitting into the tall bright cuspidors and then out again, scot-free——

The door opened behind him. Boon was wiping his mouth on the back of his hand. "All right," he said. "Let's go tend to it and get the hell out of here."

They went and had the suitcase packed. He never knew where or when Boon got the other bottle. Doubtless Mr. Semmes gave it to him. When they reached Hoke's again at sundown, it was empty. They could get a return train to Hoke's in two hours; they went straight back to the station as Major de Spain and then McCaslin had told Boon to do and then ordered him to do and had sent the boy along to see that he did. Boon took the first drink from his bottle in the washroom. A man in a uniform cap came to tell him he couldn't drink there and looked at Boon's face once and said nothing. The next time he was pouring into his water glass beneath the edge of a table in the restaurant when the manager (she was a woman) did tell him he couldn't drink there and he went back to the washroom. He had been telling the Negro waiter and all the other people in the restaurant who couldn't help but hear him and who had never heard of Lion and didn't want to, about Lion and Old Ben. Then he happened to think of the zoo. He had found out that there was another train to Hoke's at three o'clock and so they would spend the time at the zoo and take the three-o'clock train until he came back from the washroom for the third time. Then they would take the first train back to camp, get Lion and come back to the zoo where, he said, the bears were fed on ice cream and lady fingers and he would match Lion against them all.

So they missed the first train, the one they were supposed to take, but he got Boon onto the three-o'clock train and they were all right again, with Boon not even going to the wash-room now but drinking in the aisle and talking about Lion and the men he buttonholed, no more daring to tell

Boon he couldn't drink there than the man in the station had dared.

When they reached Hoke's at sundown, Boon was asleep. The boy waked him at last and got him and the suitcase off the train and he even persuaded him to eat some supper at the sawmill commissary. So he was all right when they got in the caboose of the log-train to go back into the woods, with the sun going down red and the sky already overcast and the ground would not freeze tonight. It was the boy who slept now, sitting behind the ruby stove while the springless caboose jumped and clattered and Boon and the brakeman and the conductor talked about Lion and Old Ben because they knew what Boon was talking about because this was home. "Overcast and already thawing," Boon said. "Lion will get him tomorrow."

It would have to be Lion, or somebody. It would not be Boon. He had never hit anything bigger than a squirrel that anybody ever knew, except the Negro woman that day when he was shooting at the Negro man. He was a big Negro and not ten feet away but Boon shot five times with the pistol he had borrowed from Major de Spain's Negro coachman and the Negro he was shooting at outed with a dollar-and-a-half mail-order pistol and would have burned Boon down with it only it never went off, it just went snicksnicksnicksnicksnick five times and Boon still blasting away and he broke a plate-glass window that cost McCaslin forty-five dollars and hit a Negro woman who happened to be passing in the leg only Major de Spain paid for that; he and McCaslin cut cards, the plate-glass window against the

Negro woman's leg. And the first day on stand this year, the
first morning in camp, the buck ran right over Boon; he
heard Boon's old pump gun go whow. whow. whow. whow.
whow. and then his voice: "God damn, here he comes!
Head him! Head him!" and when he got there the buck's
tracks and the five exploded shells were not twenty paces
apart.

There were five guests in camp that night, from Jefferson: Mr. Bayard Sartoris and his son and General Compson's son and two others. And the next morning he looked
out the window, into the gray thin drizzle of daybreak
which Ash had predicted, and there they were, standing
and squatting beneath the thin rain, almost two dozen of
them who had fed Old Ben corn and shoats and even
calves for ten years, in their worn hats and hunting coats
and overalls which any town Negro would have thrown
away or burned and only the rubber boots strong and
sound, and the worn and blueless guns and some even
without guns. While they ate breakfast a dozen more
arrived, mounted and on foot: loggers from the camp thirteen miles below and sawmill men from Hoke's and the
only gun among them that one which the log-train conductor carried: so that when they went into the woods this
morning Major de Spain led a party almost as strong, ex-
cepting that some of them were not armed, as some he had
led in the last darkening days of '64 and '65. The little
yard would not hold them. They overflowed it, into the
lane where Major de Spain sat his mare while Ash in his
dirty apron thrust the greasy cartridges into his carbine and

passed it up to him and the great grave blue dog stood at his stirrup not as a dog stands but as a horse stands, blinking his sleepy topaz eyes at nothing, deaf even to the yelling of the hounds which Boon and Tennie's Jim held on leash.

"We'll put General Compson on Katie this morning," Major de Spain said. "He drew blood last year; if he'd had a mule then that would have stood, he would have——"

"No," General Compson said. "I'm too old to go helling through the woods on a mule or a horse or anything else any more. Besides, I had my chance last year and missed it. I'm going on a stand this morning. I'm going to let that boy ride Katie."

"No, wait," McCaslin said. "Ike's got the rest of his life to hunt bears in. Let somebody else——"

"No," General Compson said. "I want Ike to ride Katie. He's already a better woodsman than you or me either and in another ten years he'll be as good as Walter."

At first he couldn't believe it, not until Major de Spain spoke to him. Then he was up, on the one-eyed mule which would not spook at wild blood, looking down at the dog motionless at Major de Spain's stirrup, looking in the gray streaming light bigger than a calf, bigger than he knew it actually was—the big head, the chest almost as big as his own, the blue hide beneath which the muscles flinched or quivered to no touch since the heart which drove blood to them loved no man and no thing, standing as a horse stands yet different from a horse which infers only weight and speed while Lion inferred not only courage and all else that went to make up the will and desire to pursue and kill, but endurance, the will and desire to endure beyond all imaginable limits of flesh in order to overtake and slay. Then the dog looked at him. It moved its head and looked at him across the trivial uproar of the hounds, out of the yellow eyes as depthless as Boon's, as free as Boon's of meanness or generosity or gentleness or viciousness. They were just cold and sleepy. Then it blinked, and he knew it was not looking at him and never had been, without even bothering to turn its head away.

That morning he heard the first cry. Lion had already vanished while Sam and Tennie's Jim were putting saddles on the mule and horse which had drawn the wagon and he watched the hounds as they crossed and cast, snuffing and whimpering, until they too disappeared. Then he and Major de Spain and Sam and Tennie's Jim rode after them and heard the first cry out of the wet and thawing woods not two hundred yards ahead, high, with that abject, almost human quality he had come to know, and the other hounds joining in until the gloomed woods rang and clamored. They rode then. It seemed to him that he could actually see the big blue dog boring on, silent, and the bear too: the thick, locomotive-like shape which he had seen that day four years ago crossing the blow-down, crashing on ahead of the dogs faster than he had believed it could have moved, drawing away even from the running mules. He heard a shotgun, once. The woods had opened, they were going fast, the clamor faint and fading on ahead; they passed the man who had fired—a swamper, a pointing arm, a gaunt face, the small black orifice of his yelling studded with rotten teeth.

He heard the changed note in the hounds' uproar and two hundred yards ahead he saw them. The bear had turned. He saw Lion drive in without pausing and saw the bear strike him aside and lunge into the yelling hounds and kill one of them almost in its tracks and whirl and run again. Then they were in a streaming tide of dogs. He heard Major de Spain and Tennie's Jim shouting and the pistol sound of Tennie's Jim's leather thong as he tried to turn them. Then he and Sam Fathers were riding alone. One of the hounds had kept on with Lion though. He recognized its voice. It was the young hound which even a year ago had had no judgment and which, by the lights of the other hounds anyway, still had none. *Maybe that's what courage is,* he thought. "Right," Sam said behind him. "Right. We got to turn him from the river if we can."

Now they were in cane: a brake. He knew the path through it as well as Sam did. They came out of the undergrowth and struck the entrance almost exactly. It would traverse the brake and come out onto a high open ridge above the river. He heard the flat clap of Walter Ewell's rifle, then two more. "No," Sam said. "I can hear the hound. Go on."

They emerged from the narrow roofless tunnel of snapping and hissing cane, still galloping, onto the open ridge below which the thick yellow river, reflectionless in the gray and streaming light, seemed not to move. Now he could hear the hound too. It was not running. The cry

was a high frantic yapping and Boon was running along
the edge of the bluff, his old gun leaping and jouncing
against his back on its sling made of a piece of cotton plow-
line. He whirled and ran up to them, wild-faced, and flung
himself onto the mule behind the boy. "That damn boat!"
he cried. "It's on the other side! He went straight across!
Lion was too close to him! That little hound too! Lion was
so close I couldn't shoot! Go on!" he cried, beating his
heels into the mule's flanks. "Go on!"

They plunged down the bank, slipping and sliding in
the thawed earth, crashing through the willows and into
the water. He felt no shock, no cold, he on one side of the
swimming mule, grasping the pommel with one hand and
holding his gun above the water with the other, Boon opposite him. Sam was behind them somewhere, and then the
river, the water about them, was full of dogs. They swam
faster than the mules; they were scrabbling up the bank
before the mules touched bottom. Major de Spain was
whooping from the bank they had just left and, looking
back, he saw Tennie's Jim and the horse as they went into
the water.

Now the woods ahead of them and the rain-heavy air
were one uproar. It rang and clamored; it echoed and
broke against the bank behind them and reformed and
clamored and rang until it seemed to the boy that all the
hounds which had ever bayed game in this land were yelling down at him. He got his leg over the mule as it came up
out of the water. Boon didn't try to mount again. He
grasped one stirrup as they went up the bank and crashed

through the undergrowth which fringed the bluff and saw the bear, on its hind feet, its back against a tree while the bellowing hounds swirled around it and once more Lion drove in, leaping clear of the ground.

This time the bear didn't strike him down. It caught the dog in both arms, almost loverlike, and they both went down. He was off the mule now. He drew back both hammers of the gun but he could see nothing but moiling spotted houndbodies until the bear surged up again. Boon was yelling something, he could not tell what; he could see Lion still clinging to the bear's throat and he saw the bear, half erect, strike one of the hounds with one paw and hurl it five or six feet and then, rising and rising as though it would never stop, stand erect again and begin to rake at Lion's belly with its forepaws. Then Boon was running. The boy saw the gleam of the blade in his hand and watched him leap among the hounds, hurdling them, kicking them aside as he ran, and fling himself astride the bear as he had hurled himself onto the mule, his legs locked around the bear's belly, his left arm under the bear's throat where Lion clung, and the glint of the knife as it rose and fell.

It fell just once. For an instant they almost resembled a piece of statuary: the clinging dog, the bear, the man astride its back, working and probing the buried blade. Then they went down, pulled over backward by Boon's weight, Boon underneath. It was the bear's back which reappeared first but at once Boon was astride it again. He had never released the knife and again the boy saw the almost infinitesimal movement of his arm and shoulder as he probed and sought; then the bear surged erect, raising with it the man and the dog too, and turned and still carrying the man and the dog it took two or three steps toward the woods on its hind feet as a man would have walked and crashed down. It didn't collapse, crumble. It fell all of a piece, as a tree falls, so that all three of them, man, dog and bear, seemed to bounce once.

He and Tennie's Jim ran forward. Boon was kneeling at the bear's head. His left ear was shredded, his left coat sleeve was completely gone, his right boot had been ripped from knee to instep; the bright blood thinned in the thin rain down his leg and hand and arm and down the side of his face which was no longer wild but was quite calm. Together they prized Lion's jaws from the bear's throat. "Easy, goddamn it," Boon said. "Can't you see his guts are all out of him?" He began to remove his coat. He spoke to Tennie's Jim in that calm voice: "Bring the boat up. It's about a hundred yards down the bank there. I saw it." Tennie's Jim rose and went away. Then, and he could not remember if it had been a call or an exclamation from Tennie's Jim or if he had glanced up by chance, he saw Tennie's Jim stooping and saw Sam Fathers lying motionless on his face in the trampled mud.

The mule had not thrown him. He remembered that Sam was down too even before Boon began to run. There was no mark on him whatever and when he and Boon turned him over, his eyes were open and he said something in that tongue which he and Joe Baker had used to speak together. But he couldn't move. Tennie's Jim brought the skiff up; they could hear him shouting to Major de Spain across the river. Boon wrapped Lion in his hunting coat and carried him down to the skiff and they carried Sam down and returned and hitched the bear to the one-eyed mule's saddle-bow with Tennie's Jim's leash-thong and dragged him down to the skiff and got him into it and left Tennie's Jim to swim the horse and the two mules back across. Major de Spain caught the bow of the skiff as Boon jumped out and past him before it touched the bank. He looked at Old Ben and said quietly: "Well." Then he walked into the water and leaned down and touched Sam and Sam looked up at him and said something in that old tongue he and Joe Baker spoke. "You don't know what happened?" Major de Spain said.

"No, sir," the boy said. "It wasn't the mule. It wasn't anything. He was off the mule when Boon ran in on the bear. Then we looked up and he was lying on the ground." Boon was shouting at Tennie's Jim, still in the middle of the river.

"Come on, goddamn it!" he said. "Bring me that mule!"

"What do you want with a mule?" Major de Spain said.

Boon didn't even look at him. "I'm going to Hoke's to get the doctor," he said in that calm voice, his face quite calm beneath the steady thinning of the bright blood.

"You need a doctor yourself," Major de Spain said. "Tennie's Jim——"

"Damn that," Boon said. He turned on Major de Spain.

His face was still calm, only his voice was a pitch higher. "Can't you see his goddamn guts are all out of him?"

"Boon!" Major de Spain said. They looked at one another. Boon was a good head taller than Major de Spain; even the boy was taller now than Major de Spain.

"I've got to get the doctor," Boon said. "His goddamn guts——"

"All right," Major de Spain said. Tennie's Jim came up out of the water. The horse and the sound mule had already scented Old Ben; they surged and plunged all the way up to the top of the bluff, dragging Tennie's Jim with them, before he could stop them and tie them and come back. Major de Spain unlooped the leather thong of his compass from his buttonhole and gave it to Tennie's Jim. "Go straight to Hoke's," he said. "Bring Doctor Crawford back with you. Tell him there are two men to be looked at. Take my mare. Can you find the road from here?"

"Yes, sir," Tennie's Jim said.

"All right," Major de Spain said. "Go on." He turned to the boy. "Take the mules and the horse and go back and get the wagon. We'll go on down the river in the boat to Coon bridge. Meet us there. Can you find it again?"

"Yes, sir," the boy said.

"All right. Get started."

He went back to the wagon. He realised then how far they had run. It was already afternoon when he put the mules into the traces and tied the horse's lead-rope to the tail-gate. He reached Coon bridge at dusk. The skiff was already there. Before he could see it and almost before he could see the water he had to leap from the tilting wagon, still holding the reins, and work around to where he could grasp the bit and then the ear of the plunging sound mule and dig his heels and hold it until Boon came up the bank. The rope of the lead horse had already snapped and it had already disappeared up the road toward camp. They turned the wagon around and took the mules out and he led the sound mule a hundred yards up the road and tied it. Boon had already brought Lion up to the wagon and Sam was sitting up in the skiff now and when they raised him he tried to walk, up the bank and to the wagon and he tried to climb into the wagon but Boon did not wait; he picked Sam up bodily and set him on the seat. Then they hitched Old Ben to the one-eyed mule's saddle again and dragged him up the bank and set two skid-poles into the open tail-gate and got him into the wagon and he went and got the sound mule and Boon fought it into the traces, striking it across its hard hollow-sounding face until it came into position and stood trembling. Then the rain came down, as though it had held off all day waiting on them.

They returned to camp through it, through the streaming and sightless dark, hearing long before they saw any light the horn and the spaced shots to guide them. When they came to Sam's dark little hut he tried to stand up. He spoke again in the tongue of the old fathers; then he said clearly: "Let me out. Let me out."

"He hasn't got any fire," Major said. "Go on!" he said sharply.

But Sam was struggling now, trying to stand up. "Let me out, master," he said. "Let me go home."

So he stopped the wagon and Boon got down and lifted Sam out. He did not wait to let Sam try to walk this time. He carried him into the hut and Major de Spain got light on a paper spill from the buried embers on the hearth and lit the lamp and Boon put Sam on his bunk and drew off his boots and Major de Spain covered him and the boy was not there, he was holding the mules, the sound one which was trying again to bolt since when the wagon stopped Old Ben's scent drifted forward again along the streaming blackness of air, but Sam's eyes were probably open again on that profound look which saw further than them or the hut, further than the death of a bear and the dying of a dog. Then they went on, toward the long wailing of the horn and the shots which seemed each to linger intact somewhere in the thick streaming air until the next spaced report joined and blended with it, to the lighted house, the bright streaming windows, the quiet faces as Boon entered, bloody and quite calm, carrying the bundled coat. He laid Lion, bloody coat and all, on his stale sheetless pallet bed which not even Ash, as deft in the house as a woman, could ever make smooth.

The sawmill doctor from Hoke's was already there. Boon would not let the doctor touch him until he had seen to Lion. He wouldn't risk giving Lion chloroform. He put the entrails back and sewed him up without it while Major de Spain held his head and Boon his feet. But he never tried to move. He lay there, the yellow eyes open upon nothing while the quiet men in the new hunting clothes and in the old ones crowded into the little airless room rank with the smell of Boon's body and garments, and watched. Then the doctor cleaned and disinfected Boon's face and arm and leg and bandaged them and, the boy in front with a lantern and the doctor and McCaslin and Major de Spain and General Compson following, they went to Sam Fathers' hut. Tennie's Jim had built up the fire; he squatted before it, dozing. Sam had not moved since Boon had put him in the bunk and Major de Spain had covered him with the blankets, yet he opened his eyes and looked from one to another of the faces and when McCaslin touched his shoulder and said, "Sam. The doctor wants to look at you," he even drew his hands out of the blanket and began to fumble at his shirt buttons until McCaslin said, "Wait. We'll do it." They undressed him. He lay there—the copper-brown, almost hairless body, the old man's body, the old man, the wild man not even one generation from the woods, childless, kinless, peopleless—motionless, his eyes open but no longer looking at any of them, while the doctor examined him and drew the blankets up and put the stethoscope back into his bag and snapped the bag and only the boy knew that Sam too was going to die.

"Exhaustion," the doctor said. "Shock maybe. A man his age swimming rivers in December. He'll be all right. Just make him stay in bed for a day or two. Will there be somebody here with him?"

"There will be somebody here," Major de Spain said.

They went back to the house, to the rank little room

where Boon still sat on the pallet bed with Lion's head under his hand while the men, the ones who had hunted behind Lion and the ones who had never seen him before today, came quietly in to look at him and went away. Then it was dawn and they all went out into the yard to look at Old Ben, with his eyes open too and his lips snarled back from his worn teeth and his mutilated foot and the little hard lumps under his skin which were the old bullets (there were fifty-two of them, buckshot, rifle and ball) and the single almost invisible slit under his left shoulder where Boon's blade had finally found his life. Then Ash began to beat on the bottom of the dishpan with a heavy spoon to call them to breakfast and it was the first time he could remember hearing no sound from the dogs under the kitchen while they were eating. It was as if the old bear, even dead there in the yard, was a more potent terror still than they could face without Lion between them.

The rain had stopped during the night. By midmorning the thin sun appeared, rapidly burning away mist and cloud, warming the air and the earth; it would be one of those windless Mississippi December days which are a sort of Indian summer's Indian summer. They moved Lion out to the front gallery, into the sun. It was Boon's idea. "God-damn it," he said, "he never did want to stay in the house until I made him. You know that." He took a crowbar and loosened the floor boards under his pallet bed so it could be raised, mattress and all, without disturbing Lion's position, and they carried him out to the gallery and put him down facing the woods.

Then he and the doctor and McCaslin and Major de Spain went to Sam's hut. This time Sam didn't open his eyes and his breathing was so quiet, so peaceful that they could hardly see that he breathed. The doctor didn't even take out his stethoscope nor even touch him. "He's all right," the doctor said. "He didn't even catch cold. He just quit."

"Quit?" McCaslin said.

"Yes. Old people do that sometimes. Then they get a good night's sleep or maybe it's just a drink of whisky, and they change their minds."

They returned to the house. And then they began to arrive—the swamp-dwellers, the gaunt men who ran trap-lines and lived on quinine and coons and river water, the farmers of little corn- and cotton-patches along the bottom's edge whose fields and cribs and pig-pens the old bear had rifled, the loggers from the camp and the sawmill men from Hoke's and the town men from further away than that, whose hounds the old bear had slain and traps and deadfalls he had wrecked and whose lead he carried. They came up mounted and on foot and in wagons, to enter the yard and look at him and then go on to the front where Lion lay, filling the little yard and overflowing it until there were almost a hundred of them squatting and stand-ing in the warm and drowsing sunlight, talking quietly of hunting, of the game and the dogs which ran it, of hounds and bear and deer and men of yesterday vanished from the earth, while from time to time the great blue dog would open his eyes, not as if he were listening to them but as

though to look at the woods for a moment before closing
his eyes again, to remember the woods or to see that they
were still there. He died at sundown.

Major de Spain broke camp that night. They carried
Lion into the woods, or Boon carried him that is, wrapped
in a quilt from his bed, just as he had refused to let anyone
else touch Lion yesterday until the doctor got there; Boon
carrying Lion, and the boy and General Compson and
Walter and still almost fifty of them following with lanterns
and lighted pine-knots—men from Hoke's and even further, who would have to ride out of the bottom in the dark,
and swampers and trappers who would have to walk even,
scattering toward the little hidden huts where they lived.
And Boon would let nobody else dig the grave either and
lay Lion in it and cover him and then General Compson
stood at the head of it while the blaze and smoke of the
pine-knots streamed away among the winter branches and
spoke as he would have spoken over a man. Then they returned to camp. Major de Spain and McCaslin and Ash
had rolled and tied all the bedding. The mules were
hitched to the wagon and pointed out of the bottom and
the wagon was already loaded and the stove in the kitchen
was cold and the table was set with scraps of cold food and
bread and only the coffee was hot when the boy ran into
the kitchen where Major de Spain and McCaslin had already eaten. "What?" he cried. "What? I'm not going."

"Yes," McCaslin said, "we're going out tonight. Major
wants to get on back home."

"No!" he said. "I'm going to stay."

"You've got to be back in school Monday. You've already missed a week more than I intended. It will take you from now until Monday to catch up. Sam's all right. You heard Doctor Crawford. I'm going to leave Boon and Tennie's Jim both to stay with him until he feels like getting up."

He was panting. The others had come in. He looked rapidly and almost frantically around at the other faces. Boon had a fresh bottle. He upended it and started the cork by striking the bottom of the bottle with the heel of his hand and drew the cork with his teeth and spat it out and drank. "You're damn right you're going back to school," Boon said. "Or I'll burn the tail off of you myself if Cass don't, whether you are sixteen or sixty. Where in hell do you expect to get without education? Where would Cass be? Where in hell would I be if I hadn't never went to school?"

He looked at McCaslin again. He could feel his breath coming shorter and shorter and shallower and shallower, as if there were not enough air in the kitchen for that many to breathe. "This is just Thursday. I'll come home Sunday night on one of the horses. I'll come home Sunday, then. I'll make up the time I lost studying Sunday night, McCaslin," he said, without even despair.

"No, I tell you," McCaslin said. "Sit down here and eat your supper. We're going out to——"

"Hold up, Cass," General Compson said. The boy did not know General Compson had moved until he put his hand on his shoulder. "What is it, bud?" he said.

"I've got to stay," he said. "I've got to."

"All right," General Compson said. "You can stay. If missing an extra week of school is going to throw you so far behind you'll have to sweat to find out what some hired pedagogue put between the covers of a book, you better quit altogether.—And you shut up, Cass," he said, though McCaslin had not spoken. "You've got one foot straddled into a farm and the other foot straddled into a bank; you ain't even got a good hand-hold where this boy was already an old man long before you damned Sartorises and Edmondses invented farms and banks to keep yourselves from having to find out what this boy was born knowing and fearing too maybe but without being afraid, that could go ten miles on a compass because he wanted to look at a bear none of us had ever got near enough to put a bullet in and looked at the bear and came the ten miles back on the compass in the dark; maybe by God that's the why and the wherefore of farms and banks.—I reckon you still ain't going to tell what it is?"

But still he could not. "I've got to stay," he said.

"All right," General Compson said. "There's plenty of grub left. And you'll come home Sunday, like you promised McCaslin? Not Sunday night: Sunday."

"Yes, sir," he said.

"All right," General Compson said. "Sit down and eat, boys," he said. "Let's get started. It's going to be cold before we get home."

They ate. The wagon was already loaded and ready to depart; all they had to do was to get into it. Boon would drive them out to the road, to the farmer's stable where the surrey had been left. He stood beside the wagon, in silhouette on the sky, turbaned like a Paythan and taller than any there, the bottle tilted. Then he flung the bottle from his lips without even lowering it, spinning and glinting in the faint starlight, empty. "Them that's going," he said, "get in the goddamn wagon. Them that ain't, get out of the goddamn way." The others got in. Boon mounted to the seat beside General Compson and the wagon moved, on into the obscurity until the boy could no longer see it, even the moving density of it amid the greater night. But he could still hear it, for a long while: the slow, deliberate banging of the wooden frame as it lurched from rut to rut. And he could hear Boon even when he could no longer hear the wagon. He was singing, harsh, tuneless, loud.

That was Thursday. On Saturday morning Tennie's Jim left on McCaslin's woods-horse which had not been out of the bottom one time now in six years, and late that afternoon rode through the gate on the spent horse and on to the commissary where McCaslin was rationing the tenants and the wage-hands for the coming week, and this time McCaslin forestalled any necessity or risk of having to wait while Major de Spain's surrey was being horsed and harnessed. He took their own, and with Tennie's Jim already asleep in the back seat he drove in to Jefferson and waited while Major de Spain changed to boots and put on his overcoat, and they drove the thirty miles in the dark of that night and at daybreak on Sunday morning they swapped to the waiting mare and mule and as the sun rose they rode out of the jungle and onto the low ridge where they had buried Lion: the low mound of unannealed earth where Boon's spade-marks still showed and beyond the grave the platform of freshly cut saplings bound between four posts and the blanket-wrapped bundle upon the platform and Boon and the boy squatting between the platform and the grave until Boon, the bandage removed, ripped from his head so that the long scoriations of Old Ben's claws resembled crusted tar in the sunlight, sprang up and threw down upon them with the old gun with which he had never been known to hit anything although McCaslin was already off the mule, kicked both feet free of the irons and vaulted down before the mule had stopped, walking toward Boon.

"Stand back," Boon said. "By God, you won't touch him. Stand back, McCaslin." Still McCaslin came on, fast yet without haste.

"Cass!" Major de Spain said. Then he said "Boon! You, Boon!" and he was down too and the boy rose too, quickly, and still McCaslin came on not fast but steady and walked up to the grave and reached his hand steadily out, quickly yet still not fast, and took hold the gun by the middle so that he and Boon faced one another across Lion's grave, both holding the gun, Boon's spent indomitable amazed and frantic face almost a head higher than McCaslin's beneath the black scoriations of beast's claws and then Boon's chest began to heave as though there were not enough air in all the woods, in all the wilderness, for all of them, for him and anyone else, even for him alone.

"Turn it loose, Boon," McCaslin said.

"You damn little spindling—" Boon said. "Don't you know I can take it away from you? Don't you know I can tie it around your neck like a damn cravat?"

"Yes," McCaslin said. "Turn it loose, Boon."

"This is the way he wanted it. He told us. He told us exactly how to do it. And by God you ain't going to move him. So we did it like he said, and I been sitting here ever since to keep the damn wildcats and varmints away from him and by God—" Then McCaslin had the gun, down-slanted while he pumped the slide, the five shells snicking out of it so fast that the last one was almost out before the first one touched the ground and McCaslin dropped the gun behind him without once having taken his eyes from Boon's.

"Did you kill him, Boon?" he said. Then Boon moved. He turned, he moved like he was still drunk and then for a moment blind too, one hand out as he blundered toward the big tree and seemed to stop walking before he reached the tree so that he plunged, fell toward it, flinging up both hands and catching himself against the tree and turning until his back was against it, backing with the tree's trunk his wild spent scoriated face and the tremendous heave and collapse of his chest, McCaslin following, facing him again, never once having moved his eyes from Boon's eyes. "Did you kill him, Boon?"

"No!" Boon said. "No!"

"Tell the truth," McCaslin said. "I would have done it if he had asked me to." Then the boy moved. He was be-

tween them, facing McCaslin; the water felt as if it had
burst and sprung not from his eyes alone but from his
whole face, like sweat.

"Leave him alone!" he cried. "Goddamn it! Leave him
alone!"

4. He went back to the camp one more time before
the lumber company moved in and began to cut the timber.
Major de Spain himself never saw it again. But he made
them welcome to use the house and hunt the land whenever they liked, and in the winter following the last hunt
when Sam Fathers and Lion died, General Compson and
Walter Ewell invented a plan to corporate themselves, the
old group, into a club and lease the camp and the hunting
privileges of the woods—an invention doubtless of the
somewhat childish old General but actually worthy of
Boon Hogganbeck himself. Even the boy, listening, recognised it for the subterfuge it was: to change the leopard's
spots when they could not alter the leopard, a baseless and
illusory hope to which even McCaslin seemed to subscribe
for a while, that once they had persuaded Major de Spain
to return to the camp he might revoke himself, which even
the boy knew he would not do. And he did not. The boy
never knew what occurred when Major de Spain declined.
He was not present when the subject was broached and
McCaslin never told him. But when June came and the
time for the double birthday celebration there was no mention of it and when November came no one spoke of using

Major de Spain's house and he never knew whether or
not Major de Spain knew they were going on the hunt
though without doubt old Ash probably told him: he and
McCaslin and General Compson (and that one was the
General's last hunt too) and Walter and Boon and Tennie's
Jim and old Ash loaded two wagons and drove two days
and almost forty miles beyond any country the boy had
ever seen before and lived in tents for the two weeks. And
the next spring they heard (not from Major de Spain)
that he had sold the timber-rights to a Memphis lumber
company and in June the boy came to town with McCaslin
one Saturday and went to Major de Spain's office—the big,
airy, book-lined second-storey room with windows at one
end opening upon the shabby hinder purlieus of stores and
at the other a door giving onto the railed balcony above
the Square, with its curtained alcove where sat a cedar
water-bucket and a sugar-bowl and spoon and tumbler and
a wicker-covered demijohn of whiskey, and the bamboo-
and-paper punkah swinging back and forth above the desk
while old Ash in a tilted chair beside the entrance pulled
the cord.

"Of course," Major de Spain said. "Ash will probably
like to get off in the woods himself for a while, where he
won't have to eat Daisy's cooking. Complain about it, anyway. Are you going to take anybody with you?"

"No sir," he said. "I thought that maybe Boon—" For
six months now Boon had been town-marshal at Hoke's;
Major de Spain had compounded with the lumber company—or perhaps compromised was closer, since it was the

lumber company who had decided that Boon might be better as a town-marshal than head of a logging gang.

"Yes," Major de Spain said. "I'll wire him today. He can meet you at Hoke's. I'll send Ash on by the train and they can take some food in and all you will have to do will be to mount your horse and ride over."

"Yes sir," he said. "Thank you." And he heard his voice again. He didn't know he was going to say it yet he did know, he had known it all the time: "Maybe if you . . ." His voice died. It was stopped, he never knew how because Major de Spain did not speak and it was not until his voice ceased that Major de Spain moved, turned back to the desk and the papers spread on it and even that without moving because he was sitting at the desk with a paper in his hand when the boy entered, the boy standing there looking down at the short plumpish grey-haired man in sober fine broadcloth and an immaculate glazed shirt whom he was used to seeing in boots and muddy corduroy, unshaven, sitting the shaggy powerful long-hocked mare with the worn Winchester carbine across the saddlebow and the great blue dog standing motionless as bronze at the stirrup, the two of them in that last year and to the boy anyway coming to resemble one another somehow as two people competent for love or for business who have been in love or in business together for a long time sometimes do. Major de Spain did not look up again.

"No. I will be too busy. But good luck to you. If you have it, you might bring me a young squirrel."

"Yes sir," he said. "I will."

He rode his mare, the three-year-old filly he had bred and raised and broken himself. He left home a little after midnight and six hours later, without even having sweated her, he rode into Hoke's, the tiny log-line junction which he had always thought of as Major de Spain's property too although Major de Spain had merely sold the company (and that many years ago) the land on which the sidetracks and loading-platforms and the commissary store stood, and looked about in shocked and grieved amazement even though he had had forewarning and had believed himself prepared: a new planing-mill already half completed which would cover two or three acres and what looked like miles and miles of stacked steel rails red with the light bright rust of newness and of piled crossties sharp with creosote, and wire corrals and feeding-troughs for two hundred mules at least and the tents for the men who drove them; so that he arranged for the care and stabling of his mare as rapidly as he could and did not look any more, mounted into the log-train caboose with his gun and climbed into the cupola and looked no more save toward the wall of wilderness ahead within which he would be able to hide himself from it once more anyway.

Then the little locomotive shrieked and began to move: a rapid churning of exhaust, a lethargic deliberate clashing of slack couplings traveling backward along the train, the exhaust changing to the deep slow clapping bites of power as the caboose too began to move and from the cupola he watched the train's head complete the first and only curve in the entire line's length and vanish into the

wilderness, dragging its length of train behind it so that
it resembled a small dingy harmless snake vanishing into
weeds, drawing him with it too until soon it ran once more
at its maximum clattering speed between the twin walls of
unaxed wilderness as of old. It had been harmless once.
Not five years ago Walter Ewell had shot a six-point buck
from this same moving caboose, and there was the story
of the half-grown bear: the train's first trip in to the cutting
thirty miles away, the bear between the rails, its rear end
elevated like that of a playing puppy while it dug to see
what sort of ants or bugs they might contain or perhaps
just to examine the curious symmetrical squared barkless
logs which had appeared apparently from nowhere in one
endless mathematical line overnight, still digging until the
driver on the braked engine not fifty feet away blew the
whistle at it, whereupon it broke frantically and took the
first tree it came to: an ash sapling not much bigger than
a man's thigh and climbed as high as it could and clung
there, its head ducked between its arms as a man (a woman
perhaps) might have done while the brakeman threw
chunks of ballast at it, and when the engine returned three
hours later with the first load of outbound logs the bear was
halfway down the tree and once more scrambled back up
as high as it could and clung again while the train passed
and was still there when the engine went in again in the
afternoon and still there when it came back out at dusk;
and Boon had been in Hoke's with the wagon after a barrel
of flour that noon when the train-crew told about it and
Boon and Ash, both twenty years younger then, sat under

the tree all that night to keep anybody from shooting it and the next morning Major de Spain had the log-train held at Hoke's and just before sundown on the second day, with not only Boon and Ash but Major de Spain and General Compson and Walter and McCaslin, twelve then, watching, it came down the tree after almost thirty-six hours without even water and McCaslin told him how for a minute they thought it was going to stop right there at the barrow-pit where they were standing and drink, how it looked at the water and paused and looked at them and at the water again, but did not, gone, running, as bears run, the two sets of feet, front and back, tracking two separate though parallel courses.

It had been harmless then. They would hear the passing log-train sometimes from the camp; sometimes, because nobody bothered to listen for it or not. They would hear it going in, running light and fast, the light clatter of the trucks, the exhaust of the diminutive locomotive and its shrill peanut-parcher whistle flung for one petty moment and absorbed by the brooding and inattentive wilderness without even an echo. They would hear it going out, loaded, not quite so fast now yet giving its frantic and toylike illusion of crawling speed, not whistling now to conserve steam, flinging its bitten laboring miniature puffing into the immemorial woodsface with frantic and bootless vainglory, empty and noisy and puerile, carrying to no destination or purpose sticks which left nowhere any scar or stump as the child's toy loads and transports and unloads its dead sand and rushes back for more, tireless and unceasing and rapid yet never quite so fast as the Hand which plays with it moves the toy burden back to load the toy again. But it was different now. It was the same train, engine cars and caboose, even the same enginemen brakeman and conductor to whom Boon, drunk then sober then drunk again then fairly sober once more all in the space of fourteen hours, had bragged that day two years ago about what they were going to do to Old Ben tomorrow, running with its same illusion of frantic rapidity between the same twin walls of impenetrable and impervious woods, passing the old landmarks, the old game crossings over which he had trailed bucks wounded and not wounded and more than once seen them, anything but wounded, bolt out of the woods and up and across the embankment which bore the rails and ties then down and into the woods again as the earth-bound supposedly move but crossing as arrows travel, groundless, elongated, three times its actual length and even paler, different in color, as if there were a point between immobility and absolute motion where even mass chemically altered, changing without pain or agony not only in bulk and shape but in color too, approaching the color of wind, yet this time it was as though the train (and not only the train but himself, not only his vision which had seen it and his memory which remembered it but his clothes too, as garments carry back into the clean edgeless blowing of air the lingering effluvium of a sick-room or of death) had brought with it into the doomed wilderness even before the actual axe the shadow and portent of the new mill not even finished yet and the rails and ties which were not even laid; and he knew now what he had known as soon as he saw Hoke's this morning but had not yet thought into words: why Major de Spain had not come back, and that after this time he himself, who had had to see it one time other, would return no more.

Now they were near. He knew it before the engine-driver whistled to warn him. Then he saw Ash and the wagon, the reins without doubt wrapped once more about the brake-lever as within the boy's own memory Major de Spain had been forbidding him for eight years to do, the train slowing, the slackened couplings jolting and clashing again from car to car, the caboose slowing past the wagon as he swung down with his gun, the conductor leaning out above him to signal the engine, the caboose still slowing, creeping, although the engine's exhaust was already slatting in mounting tempo against the unechoing wilderness, the crashing of draw-bars once more travelling backward along the train, the caboose picking up speed at last. Then it was gone. It had not been. He could no longer hear it. The wilderness soared, musing, inattentive, myriad, eternal, green; older than any mill-shed, longer than any spur-line. "Mr. Boon here yet?" he said.

"He beat me in," Ash said. "Had the wagon loaded and ready for me at Hoke's yistiddy when I got there and setting on the front steps at camp last night when I got in. He already been in the woods since fo daylight this morning. Said he gwine up to the Gum Tree and for you to hunt up that way and meet him." He knew where that was: a single big sweet-gum just outside the woods, in an old clearing; if you crept up to it very quietly this time of year and then ran suddenly into the clearing, sometimes you caught as many as a dozen squirrels in it, trapped, since there was no other tree near they could jump to. So he didn't get into the wagon at all.

"I will," he said.

"I figured you would," Ash said, "I fotch you a box of shells." He passed the shells down and began to unwrap the lines from the brake-pole.

"How many times up to now do you reckon Major has told you not to do that?" the boy said.

"Do which?" Ash said. Then he said: "And tell Boon Hogganbeck dinner gonter be on the table in a hour and if yawl want any to come on and eat it."

"In an hour?" he said. "It ain't nine o'clock yet." He drew out his watch and extended it face-toward Ash. "Look." Ash didn't even look at the watch.

"That's town time. You ain't in town now. You in the woods."

"Look at the sun then."

"Nemmine the sun too," Ash said. "If you and Boon Hogganbeck want any dinner, you better come on in and get it when I tole you. I aim to get done in that kitchen because I got my wood to chop. And watch your feet. They're crawling."

"I will," he said.

Then he was in the woods, not alone but solitary; the solitude closed about him, green with summer. They did not change, and, timeless, would not, any more than would

the green of summer and the fire and rain of fall and the
iron cold and sometimes even snow

the day, the morning when he killed the buck and Sam marked
his face with its hot blood, they returned to camp and he remembered old Ash's blinking and disgruntled and even outraged
disbelief until at last McCaslin had had to affirm the fact that he
had really killed it: and that night Ash sat snarling and unap-
proachable behind the stove so that Tennie's Jim had to serve
the supper and waked them with breakfast already on the table
the next morning and it was only half-past one o'clock and at last
out of Major de Spain's angry cursing and Ash's snarling and
sullen rejoinders the fact emerged that Ash not only wanted to go
into the woods and shoot a deer also but he intended to and
Major de Spain said, "By God, if we dont let him we will probably have to do the cooking from now on": and Walter Ewell
said, "Or get up at midnight to eat what Ash cooks." and since he
had already killed his buck for this hunt and was not to shoot
again unless they needed meat, he offered his gun to Ash until
Major de Spain took command and allotted that gun to Boon for
the day and gave Boon's unpredictable pump gun to Ash, with
two buckshot shells but Ash said, "I got shells:" and showed them,
four: one buck, one of number three shot for rabbits, two of bird-
shot and told one by one their history and their origin and he
remembered not Ash's face alone but Major de Spain's and
Walter's and General Compson's too, and Ash's voice: "Shoot?
In course they'll shoot! Genl Cawmpson guv me this un":—the
buckshot—"right outen the same gun he kilt that big buck with
eight years ago. And this un"—it was the rabbit shell: triumph-
antly—"is oldern thisyer boy!" And that morning he loaded the

*gun himself, reversing the order: the bird-shot, the rabbit, then
the buck so that the buckshot would feed first into the chamber,
and himself without a gun, he and Ash walked beside Major de
Spain's and Tennie's Jim's horses and the dogs (that was the
snow) until they cast and struck, the sweet strong cries ringing
away into the muffled falling air and gone almost immediately,
as if the constant and unmurmuring flakes had already buried
even the unformed echoes beneath their myriad and weightless
falling, Major de Spain and Tennie's Jim gone too, whooping on
into the woods; and then it was all right, he knew as plainly as
if Ash had told him that Ash had now hunted his deer and that
even his tender years had been forgiven for having killed one,
and they turned back toward home through the falling snow—
that is, Ash said, "Now whut?" and he said, "This way"—himself
in front because, although they were less than a mile from camp,
he knew that Ash, who had spent two weeks of his life in the
camp each year for the last twenty, had no idea whatever where
they were, until quite soon the manner in which Ash carried
Boon's gun was making him a good deal more than just nervous
and he made Ash walk in front, striding on, talking now, an old
man's garrulous monologue beginning with where he was at the
moment then of the woods and of camping in the woods and of
eating in camps then of eating then of cooking it and of his wife's
cooking then briefly of his old wife and almost at once and at
length of a new light-colored woman who nursed next door to
Major de Spain's and if she didn't watch out who she was switch-
ing her tail at he would show her how old was an old man or not
if his wife just didn't watch him all the time, the two of them in a
game trail through a dense brake of cane and brier which would*

bring them out within a quarter-mile of camp, approaching a big fallen tree-trunk lying athwart the path and just as Ash, still talking, was about to step over it the bear, the yearling, rose suddenly beyond the log, sitting up, its forearms against its chest and its wrists limply arrested as if it had been surprised in the act of covering its face to pray: and after a certain time Ash's gun yawed jerkily up and he said, "You haven't got a shell in the barrel yet. Pump it:" but the gun already snicked and he said, "Pump it. You haven't got a shell in the barrel yet:" and Ash pumped the action and in a certain time the gun steadied again and snicked and he said, "Pump it:" and watched the buckshot shell jerk, spinning heavily, into the cane. This is the rabbit shot: he thought and the gun snicked and he thought: The next is bird-shot: and he didn't have to say Pump it; he cried, "Don't shoot! Don't shoot!" but that was already too late too, the light dry vicious snick! before he could speak and the bear turned and dropped to all-fours and then was gone and there was only the log, the cane, the velvet and constant snow and Ash said, "Now whut?" and he said, "This way. Come on:" and began to back away down the path and Ash said, "I got to find my shells:" and he said, "Goddamn it, goddamn it, come on:" but Ash leaned the gun against the log and returned and stooped and fumbled among the cane roots until he came back and stooped and found the shells and they rose and at that moment the gun, untouched, leaning against the log six feet away and for that while even for-gotten by both of them, roared, bellowed and flamed, and ceased: and he carried it now, pumped out the last mummified shell and gave that one also to Ash and, the action still open, himself

carried the gun until he stood it in the corner behind Boon's bed
at the camp.

—; summer, and fall, and snow, and wet and saprife
spring in their ordered immortal sequence, the deathless
and immemorial phases of the mother who had shaped him
if any had toward the man he almost was, mother and
father both to the old man born of a Negro slave and a
Chickasaw chief who had been his spirit's father if any
had, whom he had revered and harkened to and loved
and lost and grieved: and he would marry some day and
they too would own for their brief while that brief unsub-
stanced glory which inherently of itself cannot last and
hence why glory: and they would, might, carry even the
remembrance of it into the time when flesh no longer talks
to flesh because memory at least does last: but still the
woods would be his mistress and his wife.

He was not going toward the Gum Tree. Actually he
was getting farther from it. Time was and not so long ago
either when he would not have been allowed here without
someone with him, and a little later, when he had begun
to learn how much he did not know, he would not have
dared be here without someone with him, and later still,
beginning to ascertain, even if only dimly, the limits of
what he did not know, he could have attempted and carried it through with a compass, not because of any in-
creased belief in himself but because McCaslin and Major
de Spain and Walter and General Compson too had taught
him at last to believe the compass regardless of what it
seemed to state. Now he did not even use the compass but

merely the sun and that only subconsciously, yet he could have taken a scaled map and plotted at any time to within a hundred feet of where he actually was; and sure enough, at almost the exact moment when he expected it, the earth began to rise faintly, he passed one of the four concrete markers set down by the lumber company's surveyor to establish the four corners of the plot which Major de Spain had reserved out of the sale, then he stood on the crest of the knoll itself, the four corner-markers all visible now, blanched still even beneath the winter's weathering, lifeless and shockingly alien in that place where dissolution itself was a seething turmoil of ejaculation tumescence conception and birth, and death did not even exist. After two winters' blanketings of leaves and the flood-waters of two springs, there was no trace of the two graves any more at all. But those who would have come this far to find them would not need headstones but would have found them as Sam Fathers himself had taught him to find such: by bearings on trees: and did, almost the first thrust of the hunting knife finding (but only to see if it was still there) the round tin box manufactured for axle-grease and containing now Old Ben's dried mutilated paw, resting above Lion's bones.

He didn't disturb it. He didn't even look for the other grave where he and McCaslin and Major de Spain and Boon had laid Sam's body, along with his hunting horn and his knife and his tobacco-pipe, that Sunday morning two years ago; he didn't have to. He had stepped over it, perhaps on it. But that was all right. *He probably knew I*

was in the woods this morning long before I got here, he
thought, going on to the tree which had supported one end
of the platform where Sam lay when McCaslin and Major
de Spain found them—the tree, the other axle-grease tin
nailed to the trunk, but weathered, rusted, alien too yet
healed already into the wilderness' concordant generality,
raising no tuneless note, and empty, long since empty of
the food and tobacco he had put into it that day, as empty
of that as it would presently be of this which he drew from
his pocket—the twist of tobacco, the new bandanna hand-
kerchief, the small paper sack of the peppermint candy
which Sam had used to love; that gone too, almost before
he had turned his back, not vanished but merely trans-
lated into the myriad life which printed the dark mold of
these secret and sunless places with delicate fairy tracks,
which, breathing and biding and immobile, watched him
from beyond every twig and leaf until he moved, moving
again, walking on; he had not stopped, he had only paused,
quitting the knoll which was no abode of the dead because
there was no death, not Lion and not Sam: not held fast
in earth but free in earth and not in earth but of earth,
myriad yet undiffused of every myriad part, leaf and twig
and particle, air and sun and rain and dew and night, acorn
oak and leaf and acorn again, dark and dawn and dark and
dawn again in their immutable progression and, being
myriad, one: and Old Ben too, Old Ben too; they would
give him his paw back even, certainly they would give
him his paw back: then the long challenge and the long
chase, no heart to be driven and outraged, no flesh to be

mauled and bled— Even as he froze himself, he seemed
to hear Ash's parting admonition. He could even hear the
voice as he froze, immobile, one foot just taking his weight,
the toe of the other just lifted behind him, not breathing,
feeling again and as always the sharp shocking inrush from
when Isaac McCaslin long yet was not, and so it was fear
all right but not fright as he looked down at it. It had not
coiled yet and the buzzer had not sounded either, only one
thick rapid contraction, one loop cast sideways as though
merely for purchase from which the raised head might
start slightly backward, not in fright either, not in threat
quite yet, more than six feet of it, the head raised higher
than his knee and less than his knee's length away, and old,
the once-bright markings of its youth dulled now to a
monotone concordant too with the wilderness it crawled
and lurked: the old one, the ancient and accursed about the
earth, fatal and solitary and he could smell it now: the thin
sick smell of rotting cucumbers and something else which
had no name, evocative of all knowledge and an old weari-
ness and of pariah-hood and of death. At last it moved. Not
the head. The elevation of the head did not change as it
began to glide away from him, moving erect yet off the
perpendicular as if the head and that elevated third were
complete and all: an entity walking on two feet and free of
all laws of mass and balance and should have been because
even now he could not quite believe that all that shift and
flow of shadow behind that walking head could have been
one snake: going and then gone; he put the other foot
down at last and didn't know it, standing with one hand

raised as Sam had stood that afternoon six years ago when
Sam led him into the wilderness and showed him and he
ceased to be a child, speaking the old tongue which Sam
had spoken that day without premeditation either: "Chief,"
he said: "Grandfather."

He couldn't tell when he first began to hear the sound,
because when he became aware of it, it seemed to him
that he had been already hearing it for several seconds—
a sound as though someone were hammering a gun-barrel
against a piece of railroad iron, a sound loud and heavy
and not rapid yet with something frenzied about it, as if
the hammerer were not only a strong man and an earnest
one but a little hysterical too. Yet it couldn't be on the log-
line because, although the track lay in that direction, it was
at least two miles from him and this sound was not three
hundred yards away. But even as he thought that, he
realised where the sound must be coming from: whoever
the man was and whatever he was doing, he was somewhere near the edge of the clearing where the Gum Tree
was and where he was to meet Boon. So far, he had been
hunting as he advanced, moving slowly and quietly and
watching the ground and the trees both. Now he went on,
his gun unloaded and the barrel slanted up and back to
facilitate its passage through brier and undergrowth, approaching as it grew louder and louder that steady savage
somehow queerly hysterical beating of metal on metal,
emerging from the woods, into the old clearing, with the
solitary gum tree directly before him. At first glance the
tree seemed to be alive with frantic squirrels. There ap-

peared to be forty or fifty of them leaping and darting from branch to branch until the whole tree had become one green maelstrom of mad leaves, while from time to time, singly or in twos and threes, squirrels would dart down the trunk then whirl without stopping and rush back up again as though sucked violently back by the vacuum of their fellows' frenzied vortex. Then he saw Boon, sitting, his back against the trunk, his head bent, hammering furiously at something on his lap. What he hammered with was the barrel of his dismembered gun, what he hammered at was the breech of it. The rest of the gun lay scattered about him in a half-dozen pieces while he bent over the piece on his lap his scarlet and streaming walnut face, hammering the disjointed barrel against the gun-breech with the frantic abandon of a madman. He didn't even look up to see who it was. Still hammering, he merely shouted back at the boy in a hoarse strangled voice:

"Get out of here! Don't touch them! Don't touch a one of them! They're mine!"

All that day while Issetibbeha died,
the Negro lay hidden in the barn. He was about forty,
a Guinea man. He had been taken at fourteen by a
trader off Kamerun before his teeth were filed. He had
been the Chief's body servant for twenty-three years.
    As soon as it was dark, he began to run. He knew the
country well because he had hunted it often with
Issetibbeha, following on his mule the course of the fox
or the cat (sometimes even a bear come up from the
Big Bottom along the river) beside Issetibbeha's mare;
he knew it as well as the men who would pursue him.
He saw them for the first time shortly before sunset on
the second day. He had run thirty miles then, up the
creek, before doubling back; lying in a pawpaw thicket
he saw the pursuers for the first time. There were two of
them, in shirts and straw hats, carrying their neatly-rolled

trousers under their arms, and they had no weapons. They were middle-aged, paunchy, and they could not have moved very fast anyway; it would be twelve hours before they could return to where he lay watching them. "So I will have until midnight to rest," he said. He was near enough to the plantation to smell the cooking fires, and he thought how he ought to be hungry, since he had not eaten in thirty hours. "But it is more important to rest," he told himself. He continued to tell himself that, lying in the pawpaw thicket, because the effort of resting, the need and the haste to rest, made his heart thud the same as the running had done. It was as though he had forgot how to rest, as though the six hours were not long enough to do it in, to remember again how to do it.

As soon as dark came he moved again. He had thought to keep going steadily and quietly through the night, since there was nowhere for him to go, but as soon as he moved he began to run at top speed, breasting his panting chest, his broad-flaring nostrils through the choked and whipping darkness. He ran for an hour, lost by then, without direction, when suddenly he stopped, and after a time his thudding heart unraveled from the sound of the drums. By the sound they were not two miles away; he followed the sound until he could smell the smudge fire and taste the acrid smoke. When he stood among them the drums did not cease; only the headman

came to him where he stood in the drifting smudge,
panting, his nostrils flaring and pulsing, the hushed glare
of his ceaseless eyeballs in his mud-daubed face as
though they were worked from lungs. The headman was
a Guinea man too and could have been his father, as
some of the others watching him could have been his
sons; and all of them, Guinea or not, had been his
brothers until that moment two days ago when Issetibbeha
died, now irrevocable and alien to him, of another race,
another world, another time.

"We have expected thee," the headman said. "Eat,
and go. The living may not consort with the dead. Thou
knowest that."

"Yes," he said. "I know that. They did not look at one
another. The drums had not ceased.

"Will thou eat?" the headman said.

"I am not hungry. I caught a rabbit this afternoon, and
ate while I lay hidden."

"Take some cooked meat with thee, then."

He accepted the cooked meat, wrapped in leaves, and
entered the creek bottom; after a while the sound
of the drums ceased. He walked steadily until daybreak.
"I have twelve hours," he said. "Maybe more, since
the trail was followed by night." He squatted and ate the
meat and wiped his hands on his thighs. Then he rose
and removed the dungaree pants and squatted again
beside a slough and coated himself with mud—face,

arms, body and legs—and squatted again, clasping his knees, his head bowed. When it was light enough to see, he moved back into the swamp and squatted again and went to sleep so. He did not dream at all. It was well that he moved, for, waking suddenly in broad daylight and the high sun, he saw the two Indians. They still carried their neatly rolled trousers; they stood opposite the place where he lay hidden, paunchy, thick, soft-looking, a little ludicrous in their straw hats and shirt tails.

"Damn that Negro," one of them said.

"Damn all of them," the other said. "Maybe Moketubbe will free them now. When have they ever been anything but a trouble to us?"

He ran again then, rested and refreshed; at noon, from the top of a tree, he looked down into the plantation. He could see Issetibbeha's body in a hammock between the two trees where the horse and the dog were tethered, and the concourse about the steamboat-house was filled with wagons and horses and mules, with carts and saddle-horses, while in bright clumps the women and smaller children and the old men squatted about the long trench where the smoke from the barbecuing meat blew slow and thick. The men and the big boys would all be down there in the creek bottom behind him, on the trail, their Sunday clothes rolled carefully up and wedged into tree crotches. There was a clump of men near the

*front door though, and then he saw them bring
Moketubbe himself out in a litter made of buckskin and
persimmon poles—Moketubbe, a creature so gross with
fat that it was almost necessary to carry him from bed
to table to latrine. "Yao," the Negro said quietly. "He
will go too, then. That man whose body has been dead
for fifteen years, he will go also." It was as though for the
first time he realised his true situation, how desperate,
how irrevocable, how doomed.*

*He ran again. In the middle of the afternoon he came
face to face with one of them. They were both on a
footlog across a slough—the Negro gaunt, lean, hard,
tireless and desperate; the Indian thick, soft-looking, the
apparent embodiment of the supreme reluctance and
inertia. The Indian made no move, no sound; he stood
on the log and watched the Negro plunge down into
the slough and swim ashore and crash away into the
undergrowth.*

*Just before sunset he lay behind a down log. Up the
log in slow procession moved a line of ants. He caught
them and ate them slowly, with a kind of detachment, like
that of a dinner guest eating salted nuts from a dish.
They too had a salt taste, engendering a salivary reaction
out of all proportion. He ate them slowly, watching the
unbroken line move up the log and into oblivious doom
with a steady and terrific undeviation. He had eaten
nothing else all day; in his caked mud mask his eyes*

rolled in reddened rims. At sunset, creeping along the creek bank toward where he had spotted a frog, a cottonmouth moccasin slashed him suddenly across the forearm with a thick, sluggish blow. It struck clumsily, leaving two long slashes across his arm like two razor slashes, and half sprawled with its own momentum and rage, it appeared for the moment utterly helpess with its own awkwardness and choleric anger. "Olé, Grandfather," the Negro said. He touched its head and watched it slash him again across his arm, and again, with thick, raking, awkward blows. "It's that I do not wish to die," he said. Then he said it again—"It's that I do not wish to die"—in a quiet tone, of slow and low amaze, as though it were something that, until the words had said themselves, he found that he had not known, or had not known the depth and extent of his desire.

That was when he really knew that he was lost. First he had to find a place of secrecy and security when the sickness came. It was deep in the swamp, where he could efface his trail behind him. At first the arm swelled so rapidly that the mud cracked off as fast as he plastered it on. But by the next night the swelling had stopped and even the sickness had begun to pass. And that was when the arm began to smell. He thought of running again; he could run again now. But that would be making a free gift of his presence to any of the pursuers whom he happened to pass up-wind, while here one of them would

*have to locate him by chance and scent him down. And
he thought of an axe or hatchet, to cut the arm off and
bury it, thinking, trying to remember something from the
dim time of the grass huts beyond the terrible ordeal of
the ship, when all the people were his people, using the
excruciatingly contrived edges of the bones of huge beasts
to cut with. Then that went too; he could not hold that
long enough either. And now he knew that it was the
waiting and that night he crept out; he had not heard
them but he knew they were there and in the dark he
could smell their fear too; he stood erect then, shouting
at them in the darkness: "Yao. Come and take me. Why
are you afraid?"*

*But it was dawn when two of them entered the swamp.
When he heard them, he began to sing. He knew that
they could see him now, naked and mudcaked, sitting on
a log, because he could see them too, squatting a short
distance away, until he had finished. Then one of them
rose (it was Three Basket, one of Issetibbeha's chief
counselors and who, if Issetibbeha had had his way,
would have been his successor) and came and touched
him on the arm. "Come," Basket said. "You ran well.
Do not be ashamed."*

*As they neared the plantation in the tainted bright
morning, the Negro's eyes began to roll a little, like those
of a horse. The smoke from the cooking pit blew low
along the earth and upon the squatting and waiting*

*guests about the yard and upon the steamboat deck, in
their bright, stiff, harsh finery; the women, the children,
the old men. They had sent couriers along the bottom,
and another on ahead, and Issetibbeha's body had already
been removed to where the grave waited, along with the
horse and the dog, though they could still smell him in
death about the house where he had lived in life. The
guests were beginning to move toward the grave when the
bearers of Moketubbe's litter mounted the slope.*

*The Negro was the tallest there, his high, close,
mud-caked head looming above them all. He was
breathing hard, as though the desperate effort of the six
suspended and desperate days had catapulted upon him
at once; although they walked slowly, his naked scarred
chest rose and fell above the close-clutched left arm. He
looked this way and that continuously, as if he were not
seeing, as though sight never quite caught up with the
looking. His mouth was open a little upon his big white
teeth; he began to pant. The already moving guests
halted, pausing, looking back, some with pieces of meat
in their hands, as the Negro looked about at their faces
with his wild, restrained, unceasing eyes.*

*"Will you eat first?" Basket said. He had to say it
twice.*

"Yes," the Negro said. "That's it. I want to eat."

*The throng had begun to press back toward the center;
the word passed to the outermost: "He will eat first."*

They reached the steamboat. "Sit down," Basket said. The Negro sat on the edge of the deck. He was still panting, his chest rising and falling, his head ceaseless with its white eyeballs, turning from side to side. It was as if the inability to see came from within, from hopelessness, not from absence of vision. They brought food and watched quietly as he tried to eat it. He put the food into his mouth and chewed it, but chewing, the half-masticated matter began to emerge from the corners of his mouth and to drool down his chin, onto his chest, and after a while he stopped chewing and sat there, naked, covered with dried mud, the plate on his knees, and his mouth filled with a mass of chewed food, open, his eyes wide and unceasing, panting and panting. They watched him, patient, implacable, waiting.

"Come," Basket said at last.

"It's water I want," the Negro said. "I want water."

The well was a little way down the slope toward the quarters. The slope lay dappled with the shadows of noon, of that peaceful hour when, Issetibbeha napping in his chair and waiting for the noon meal and the long afternoon to sleep in, the Negro, the body servant, would be free. He would sit in the kitchen door then, talking with the women who prepared the food. Beyond the kitchen the lane between the quarters would be quiet, peaceful, with the women talking to one another across the lane and the smoke of the dinner fires blowing upon the pickaninnies like ebony toys in the dust.

"Come," Basket said.

The Negro walked among them, taller than any. The guests were moving on toward where Issetibbeha and the horse and the dog waited. The Negro walked with his high ceaseless head, his panting chest. "Come," Basket said. "You wanted water."

"Yes," the Negro said. "Yes." He looked back at the house, then down to the quarters, where today no fire burned, no face showed in any door, no pickaninny in the dust, panting. "It struck me here, raking me across this arm; once, twice, three times. I said, 'Olé, Grandfather.'"

"Come now," Basket said. The Negro was still going through the motion of walking, his knee action high, his head high, as though he were on a treadmill. His eyeballs had a wild, restrained glare, like those of a horse. "You wanted water," Basket said. "Here it is."

There was a gourd in the well. They dipped it full and gave it to the Negro, and they watched him try to drink. His eyes had not ceased as he tilted the gourd slowly against his caked face. They could watch his throat working and the bright water cascading from either side of the gourd, down his chin and breast. Then the water stopped. "Come," Basket said.

"Wait," the Negro said. He dipped the gourd again and tilted it against his face, beneath his ceaseless eyes. Again

*they watched his throat working and the unswallowed
water sheathing broken and myriad down his chin,
channeling his caked chest. They waited, patient, grave,
decorous, implacable; clansman and guest and kin.
Then the water ceased, though still the empty gourd
tilted higher and higher, and still his black throat aped
the vain motion of his frustrated swallowing. A piece of
water-loosened mud carried away from his chest and
broke at his muddy feet, and in the empty gourd they
could hear his breath: ah-ah-ah.*

*"Come," Basket said, taking the gourd from the Negro
and hanging it back in the well.*

2

THE
OLD PEOPLE

1. At first there was nothing. There was the faint, cold, steady rain, the gray and constant light of the late November dawn, with the voices of the hounds converging somewhere in it and toward them. Then Sam Fathers, standing just behind the boy as he had been standing when the boy shot his first running rabbit with his first gun and almost with the first load it ever carried, touched his shoulder and he began to shake, not with any cold. Then the buck was there. He did not come into sight; he was just there, looking not like a ghost but as if all of light were condensed in him and he were the source of it, not only moving in it but disseminating it, already running, seen first as you always see the deer, in that split second after he has already seen you, already slanting away in that first soaring bound, the antlers even in that dim light looking like a small rocking-chair balanced on his head.

"Now," Sam Fathers said, "shoot quick, and slow."

The boy did not remember that shot at all. He would live to be eighty, as his father and his father's twin brother and their father in his turn had lived to be, but he would never hear that shot nor remember even the shock of the gun-butt. He didn't even remember what he did with the gun afterward. He was running. Then he was standing over the buck where it lay on the wet earth still in the attitude of speed and not looking at all dead, standing over it shaking and jerking, with Sam Fathers beside him again, extending the knife. "Don't walk up to him in front," Sam said. "If he ain't dead, he will cut you all to pieces with his feet. Walk up to him

from behind and take him by the horn first, so you can hold
his head down until you can jump away. Then slip your
other hand down and hook your fingers in his nostrils."

The boy did that—drew the head back and the throat
taut and drew Sam Fathers' knife across the throat and Sam
stooped and dipped his hands in the hot smoking blood and
wiped them back and forth across the boy's face. Then Sam's
horn rang in the wet gray woods and again and again; there
was a boiling wave of dogs about them, with Tennie's Jim
and Boon Hogganbeck whipping them back after each had
had a taste of the blood, then the men, the true hunters—
Walter Ewell whose rifle never missed, and Major de Spain
and old General Compson and the boy's cousin, McCaslin
Edmonds, grandson of his father's sister, sixteen years his
senior and, since both he and McCaslin were only children
and the boy's father had been nearing seventy when he was
born, more his brother than his cousin and more his father
than either—sitting their horses and looking down at them:
at the old man of seventy who had been a Negro for two
generations now but whose face and bearing were still those
of the Chickasaw chief who had been his father; and the
white boy of twelve with the prints of the bloody hands on
his face, who had nothing to do now but stand straight and
not let the trembling show.

"Did he do all right, Sam?" his cousin McCaslin said.

"He done all right," Sam Fathers said.

They were the white boy, marked forever, and the old
dark man sired on both sides by savage kings, who had
marked him, whose bloody hands had merely formally con-

secrated him to that which, under the man's tutelage, he had already accepted, humbly and joyfully, with abnegation and with pride too; the hands, the touch, the first worthy blood which he had been found at last worthy to draw, joining him and the man forever, so that the man would continue to live past the boy's seventy years and then eighty years, long after the man himself had entered the earth as chiefs and kings entered it—the child, not yet a man, whose grandfather had lived in the same country and in almost the same manner as the boy himself would grow up to live, leaving his descendants in the land in his turn as his grandfather had done, and the old man past seventy whose grandfathers had owned the land long before the white men ever saw it and who had vanished from it now with all their kind, what of blood they left behind them running now in another race and for a while even in bondage and now drawing toward the end of its alien and irrevocable course, barren, since Sam Fathers had no children.

His father was Ikkemotubbe himself, who had named himself Doom. Sam told the boy about that—how Ikkemotubbe, old Issetibbeha's sister's son, had run away to New Orleans in his youth and returned seven years later with a French companion calling himself the Chevalier Soeur-Blonde de Vitry, who must have been the Ikkemotubbe of his family too and who was already addressing Ikkemotubbe as *Du Homme*—returned, came home again, with his foreign Aramis and the quadroon slave woman who was to be Sam's mother, and a gold-laced hat and coat and a wicker wine-hamper containing a litter of month-old puppies and a gold snuff-box filled with a white powder resembling fine sugar. And how he was met at the River landing by three or four companions of his bachelor youth, and while the light of a smoking torch gleamed on the glittering braid of the hat and coat Doom squatted in the mud of the land and took one of the puppies from the hamper and put a pinch of the white powder on its tongue and the puppy died before the one who was holding it could cast it away. And how they returned to the Plantation where Issetibbeha, dead now, had been succeeded by his son, Doom's fat cousin Moketubbe, and the next day Moketubbe's eight-year-old son died suddenly and that afternoon, in the presence of Moketubbe and most of the others (the People, Sam Fathers called them) Doom produced another puppy from the wine-hamper and put a pinch of the white powder on its tongue and Moketubbe abdicated and Doom became in fact The Man which his French friend already called him. And how on the day after that, during the ceremony of accession, Doom pronounced a marriage between the pregnant quadroon and one of the slave men which he had just inherited (that was how Sam Fathers got his name, which in Chickasaw had been Had-Two-Fathers) and two years later sold the man and woman and the child who was his own son to his white neighbor, Carothers McCaslin.

That was seventy years ago. The Sam Fathers whom the boy knew was already sixty—a man not tall, squat rather, almost sedentary, flabby-looking though he actually was not, with hair like a horse's mane which even at seventy showed no trace of white and a face which showed no age until he smiled, whose only visible trace of Negro blood was a slight dullness of the hair and the fingernails, and something else which you did notice about the eyes, which you noticed because it was not always there, only in repose and not always then—something not in their shape nor pigment but in their expression, and the boy's cousin McCaslin told him what that was: not the heritage of Ham, not the mark of servitude but of bondage; the knowledge that for a while that part of his blood had been the blood of slaves. "Like an old lion or a bear in a cage," McCaslin said. "He was born in the cage and has been in it all his life; he knows nothing else. Then he smells something. It might be anything, any breeze blowing past anything and then into his nostrils. But there for a second was the hot sand or the cane-brake that he never even saw himself, might not even know if he did see it and probably does know he couldn't hold his own with it if he got back to it. But that's not what he smells then. It was the cage he smelled. He hadn't smelled the cage until that minute. Then the hot sand or the brake blew into his nostrils and blew away, and all he could smell was the cage. That's what makes his eyes look like that."

"Then let him go!" the boy cried. "Let him go!"

His cousin laughed shortly. Then he stopped laughing, making the sound that is. It had never been laughing. "His cage ain't McCaslin's," he said. "He was a wild man. When he was born, all his blood on both sides, except the little white part, knew things that had been tamed out of our blood so long ago that we have not only forgotten them, we have to live together in herds to protect ourselves from our own sources. He was the direct son not only of a warrior but of a chief. Then he grew up and began to learn things, and all of a sudden one day he found out that he had been betrayed, the blood of the warriors and chiefs had been betrayed. Not by his father," he added quickly. "He probably never held it against old Doom for selling him and his mother into slavery, because he probably believed the damage was already done before then and it was the same warriors' and chiefs' blood in him and Doom both that was betrayed through the black blood which his mother gave him. Not betrayed by the black blood and not wilfully betrayed by his mother, but betrayed by her all the same, who had bequeathed him not only the blood of slaves but even a little of the very blood which had enslaved it; himself his own battleground, the scene of his own vanquishment and the mausoleum of his defeat. His cage ain't us," McCaslin said. "Did you ever know anybody yet, even your father and Uncle Buddy, that ever told him to do or not do anything that he ever paid any attention to?"

That was true. The boy first remembered him as sitting in the door of the plantation blacksmith-shop, where he sharpened plow-points and mended tools and even did rough carpenter-work when he was not in the woods. And sometimes, even when the woods had not drawn him, even with the shop cluttered with work which the farm waited on, Sam would sit there, doing nothing at all for half a day or a whole one, and no man, neither the boy's father and twin uncle in their day nor his cousin McCaslin after he became practical though not yet titular master, ever to say to him,

"I want this finished by sundown" or "Why wasn't this done yesterday?" And once each year, in the late fall, in November, the boy would watch the wagon, the hooped canvas top erected now, being loaded—the food, hams and sausage from the smokehouse, coffee and flour and molasses from the commissary, a whole beef killed just last night for the dogs until there would be meat in camp, the crate containing the dogs themselves, then the bedding, the guns, the horns and lanterns and axes, and his cousin McCaslin and Sam Fathers in their hunting clothes would mount to the seat and with Tennie's Jim sitting on the dog-crate they would drive away to Jefferson, to join Major de Spain and General Compson and Boon Hogganbeck and Walter Ewell and go on into the big bottom of the Tallahatchie where the deer and bear were, to be gone two weeks. But before the wagon was even loaded the boy would find that he could watch no longer. He would go away, running almost, to stand behind the corner where he could not see the wagon and nobody could see him, not crying, holding himself rigid except for the trembling, whispering to himself: "Soon now. Soon now. Just three more years" (or two more or one more) "and I will be ten. Then Cass said I can go."

White man's work, when Sam did work. Because he did nothing else: farmed no allotted acres of his own, as the other ex-slaves of old Carothers McCaslin did, performed no field-work for daily wages as the younger and newer Negroes did —and the boy never knew just how that had been settled between Sam and old Carothers, or perhaps with old Carothers' twin sons after him. For, although Sam lived among the Negroes, in a cabin among the other cabins in the quarters, and consorted with Negroes (what of consorting with anyone Sam did after the boy got big enough to walk alone from the house to the blacksmith-shop and then to carry a gun) and dressed like them and talked like them and even went with them to the Negro church now and then, he was still the son of that Chickasaw chief and the Negroes knew it. And, it seemed to the boy, not only Negroes. Boon Hogganbeck's grandmother had been a Chickasaw woman too, and although the blood had run white since and Boon was a white man, it was not chief's blood. To the boy at least, the difference was apparent immediately you saw Boon and Sam together, and even Boon seemed to know it was there—even Boon, to whom in his tradition it had never occurred that anyone might be better born than himself. A man might be smarter, he admitted that, or richer (luckier, he called it) but not better born. Boon was a mastiff, absolutely faithful, dividing his fidelity equally between Major de Spain and the boy's cousin McCaslin, absolutely dependent for his very bread and dividing that impartially too between Major de Spain and McCaslin, hardy, generous, courageous enough, a slave to all the appetites and almost unratiocinative. In the boy's eyes at least it was Sam Fathers, the Negro, who bore himself not only toward his cousin McCaslin and Major de Spain but toward all white men, with gravity and dignity and without servility or recourse to that impenetrable wall of ready and easy mirth which Negroes sustain between themselves and white men, bearing himself toward his cousin McCaslin not only as one man to another but as an older man to a younger.

He taught the boy the woods, to hunt, when to shoot and when not to shoot, when to kill and when not to kill, and better, what to do with it afterward. Then he would talk to the boy, the two of them sitting beneath the close fierce stars on a summer hilltop while they waited for the hounds to bring the fox back within hearing, or beside a fire in the November or December woods while the dogs worked out a coon's trail along the creek, or fireless in the pitch dark and heavy dew of April mornings while they squatted beneath a turkey-roost. The boy would never question him; Sam did not react to questions. The boy would just wait and then listen and Sam would begin, talking about the old days and the People whom he had not had time ever to know and so could not remember (he did not remember ever having seen his father's face), and in place of whom the other race into which his blood had run supplied him with no substitute.

And as he talked about those old times and those dead and vanished men of another race from either that the boy knew, gradually to the boy those old times would cease to be old time and would become a part of the boy's present, not only as if they had happened yesterday but as if they were still happening, the men who walked through them actually walking in breath and air and casting an actual shadow on the earth they had not quitted. And more: as if some of them had not happened yet but would occur tomorrow, until at last it would seem to the boy that he himself had not come into existence yet, that none of his race nor the other subject race which his people had brought with them into the land had come here yet; that although it had been his grandfather's and then his father's and uncle's and was now his cousin's and some day would be his own land which he and Sam hunted over, their hold upon it actually was as trivial and without reality as the now faded and archaic script in the chancery book in Jefferson which allocated it to them and that it was he, the boy, who was the guest here and Sam Father's voice the mouthpiece of the host.

Until three years ago there had been two of them, the other a full-blood Chickasaw, in a sense even more incredibly lost than Sam Fathers. He called himself Jobaker, as if it were one word. Nobody knew his history at all. He was a hermit, living in a foul little shack at the forks of the creek five miles from the plantation and about that far from any other habitation. He was a market hunter and fisherman and he consorted with nobody, black or white; no Negro would even cross his path and no man dared approach his hut except Sam. And perhaps once a month the boy would find them in Sam's shop—two old men squatting on their heels on the dirt floor, talking in a mixture of negroid English and flat hill dialect and now and then a phrase of that old tongue which as time went on and the boy squatted there too listening, he began to learn. Then Jobaker died. That is, nobody had seen him in some time. Then one morning Sam was missing, nobody, not even the boy, knew when nor where, until that night when some Negroes hunting in the creek bottom saw the sudden burst of flame and approached. It was Jobaker's hut, but before they got anywhere near it, someone shot at them from the shadows beyond it. It was Sam who fired, but nobody ever found Jobaker's grave.

The next morning, sitting at breakfast with his cousin, the boy saw Sam pass the dining-room window and he remembered then that never in his life before had he seen Sam nearer the house than the blacksmith-shop. He stopped eating even; he sat there and he and his cousin both heard the voices from beyond the pantry door, then the door opened and Sam entered, carrying his hat in his hand but without knocking as anyone else on the place except a house servant would have done, entered just far enough for the door to close behind him and stood looking at neither of them—the Indian face above the nigger clothes, looking at something over their heads or at something not even in the room.

"I want to go," he said. "I want to go to the Big Bottom to live."

"To live?" the boy's cousin said.

"At Major de Spain's and your camp, where you go to hunt," Sam said. "I could take care of it for you all while you ain't there. I will build me a little house in the woods, if you rather I didn't stay in the big one."

"What about Isaac here?" his cousin said. "How will you get away from him? Are you going to take him with you?" But still Sam looked at neither of them, standing just inside the room with that face which showed nothing, which showed that he was an old man only when it smiled.

"I want to go," he said. "Let me go."

"Yes," the cousin said quietly. "Of course. I'll fix it with Major de Spain. You want to go soon?"

"I'm going now," Sam said. He went out. And that was all. The boy was nine then; it seemed perfectly natural that nobody, not even his cousin McCaslin, should argue with Sam. Also, since he was nine now, he could understand that Sam could leave him and their days and nights in the woods together without any wrench. He believed that he and Sam both knew that this was not only temporary but that the exigencies of his maturing, of that for which Sam had been training him all his life some day to dedicate himself, required it. They had settled that one night last summer while they listened to the hounds bringing a fox back up the creek valley; now the boy discerned in that very talk under the high, fierce August stars a presage, a warning, of this moment today. "I done taught you all there is of this settled country," Sam said. "You can hunt it good as I can now. You are ready for the Big Bottom now, for bear and deer. Hunter's meat," he said. "Next year you will be ten. You will write your age in two numbers and you will be ready to become a man. Your pa" (Sam always referred to the boy's cousin as his father, establishing even before the boy's orphanhood did that relation between them not of the ward to his guardian and kinsman and chief and head of his blood, but of the child to the man who sired his flesh and his thinking too) "promised you can go with us then." So the boy could understand Sam's going. But he couldn't understand why now, in March, six months before the moon for hunting.

"If Jobaker's dead like they say," he said, "and Sam hasn't got anybody but us at all kin to him, why does he want to

go to the Big Bottom now, when it will be six months before
we get there?"

"Maybe that's what he wants," McCaslin said. "Maybe
he wants to get away from you a little while."

But that was all right. McCaslin and other grown people
often said things like that and he paid no attention to them,
just as he paid no attention to Sam saying he wanted to go to
the Big Bottom to live. After all, he would have to live there
for six months, because there would be no use in going at
all if he was going to turn right around and come back. And,
as Sam himself had told him, he already knew all about
hunting in this settled country that Sam or anybody else
could teach him. So it would be all right. Summer, then the
bright days after the first frost, then the cold and himself on
the wagon with McCaslin this time and the moment would
come and he would draw the blood, the big blood which
would make him a man, a hunter, and Sam would come back
home with them and he too would have outgrown the
child's pursuit of rabbits and 'possums. Then he too would
make one before the winter fire, talking of the old hunts
and the hunts to come as hunters talked.

So Sam departed. He owned so little that he could carry
it. He walked. He would neither let McCaslin send him in
the wagon, nor take a mule to ride. No one saw him go even.
He was just gone one morning, the cabin which had never
had very much in it, vacant and empty, the shop in which
there never had been very much done, standing idle. Then
November came at last, and now the boy made one—himself and his cousin McCaslin and Tennie's Jim, and Major

de Spain and General Compson and Walter Ewell and Boon and old Uncle Ash to do the cooking, waiting for them in Jefferson with the other wagon, and the surrey in which he and McCaslin and General Compson and Major de Spain would ride.

Sam was waiting at the camp to meet them. If he was glad to see them, he did not show it. And if, when they broke camp two weeks later to return home, he was sorry to see them go, he did not show that either. Because he did not come back with them. It was only the boy who returned, returning solitary and alone to the settled familiar land, to follow for eleven months the childish business of rabbits and such while he waited to go back, having brought with him, even from his brief first sojourn, an unforgettable sense of the big woods—not a quality dangerous or particularly inimical, but profound, sentient, gigantic and brooding, amid which he had been permitted to go to and fro at will, unscathed, why he knew not, but dwarfed and, until he had drawn honorably blood worthy of being drawn, alien.

Then November, and they would come back. Each morning Sam would take the boy out to the stand allotted him. It would be one of the poorer stands of course, since he was only ten and eleven and twelve and he had never even seen a deer running yet. But they would stand there, Sam a little behind him and without a gun himself, as he had been standing when the boy shot the running rabbit when he was eight years old. They would stand there in the November dawns, and after a while they would hear the dogs. Sometimes the chase would sweep up and past quite close, belling and invisible; once they heard the two heavy reports of Boon Hogganbeck's old gun with which he had never killed anything larger than a squirrel and that sitting, and twice they heard the flat unreverberant clap of Walter Ewell's rifle, following which you did not even wait to hear his horn.

"I'll never get a shot," the boy said. "I'll never kill one."

"Yes you will," Sam said. "You wait. You'll be a hunter. You'll be a man."

But Sam wouldn't come out. They would leave him there. He would come as far as the road where the surrey waited, to take the riding horses back, and that was all. The men would ride the horses and Uncle Ash and Tennie's Jim and the boy would follow in the wagon with Sam, with the camp equipment and the trophies, the meat, the heads, the antlers, the good ones, the wagon winding on among the tremendous gums and cypresses and oaks where no axe save that of the hunter had ever sounded, between the impenetrable walls of cane and brier—the two changing yet constant walls just beyond which the wilderness whose mark he had brought away forever on his spirit even from that first two weeks seemed to lean, stooping a little, watching them and listening, not quite inimical because they were too small, even those such as Walter and Major de Spain and old General Compson who had killed many deer and bear, their sojourn too brief and too harmless to excite to that, but just brooding, secret, tremendous, almost inattentive.

Then they would emerge, they would be out of it, the line as sharp as the demarcation of a doored wall. Suddenly skeleton cotton- and corn-fields would flow away on either hand, gaunt and motionless beneath the gray rain; there would be a house, barns, fences, where the hand of man had clawed for an instant, holding, the wall of the wilderness behind them now, tremendous and still and seemingly impenetrable in the gray and fading light, the very tiny orifice through which they had emerged apparently swallowed up. The surrey would be waiting, his cousin McCaslin and Major de Spain and General Compson and Walter and Boon dismounted beside it. Then Sam would get down from the wagon and mount one of the horses and, with the others on a rope behind him, he would turn back. The boy would watch him for a while against that tall and secret wall, growing smaller and smaller against it, never looking back. Then he would enter it, returning to what the boy believed, and thought that his cousin McCaslin believed, was his loneliness and solitude.

2. So the instant came. He pulled trigger and Sam Fathers marked his face with the hot blood which he had spilled and he ceased to be a child and became a hunter and a man. It was the last day. They broke camp that afternoon and went out, his cousin and Major de Spain and General Compson and Boon on the horses, Walter Ewell and the Negroes in the wagon with him and Sam and his hide and antlers. There could have been (and were) other trophies in the wagon. But for him they did not exist, just as for all practical purposes he and Sam Fathers were still alone together as they had been that morning. The wagon wound

and jolted between the slow and shifting yet constant walls from beyond and above which the wilderness watched them pass, less than inimical now and never to be inimical again since the buck still and forever leaped, the shaking gun-barrels coming constantly and forever steady at last, crashing, and still out of his instant of immortality the buck sprang, forever immortal; the wagon jolting and bouncing on, the moment of the buck, the shot, Sam Fathers and himself and the blood with which Sam had marked him forever one with the wilderness which had accepted him since Sam said that he had done all right, when suddenly Sam reined back and stopped the wagon and they all heard the unmistakable and unforgettable sound of a deer breaking cover.

Then Boon shouted from beyond the bend of the trail and while they sat motionless in the halted wagon, Walter and the boy already reaching for their guns, Boon came galloping back, flogging his mule with his hat, his face wild and amazed as he shouted down at them. Then the other riders came around the bend, also spurring.

"Get the dogs!" Boon cried. "Get the dogs! If he had a nub on his head, he had fourteen points! Laying right there by the road in that pawpaw thicket! If I'd a knowed he was there, I could have cut his throat with my pocket knife!"

"Maybe that's why he run," Walter said. "He saw you never had your gun." He was already out of the wagon with his rifle. Then the boy was out too with his gun, and the other riders came up and Boon got off his mule somehow and was scrabbling and clawing among the duffel in the wagon, still shouting, "Get the dogs! Get the dogs!" And it seemed to the boy too that it would take them forever to decide what to do—the old men in whom the blood ran cold and slow, in whom during the intervening years between them and himself the blood had become a different and colder substance from that which ran in him and even in Boon and Walter.

"What about it, Sam?" Major de Spain said. "Could the dogs bring him back?"

"We won't need the dogs," Sam said. "If he don't hear the dogs behind him, he will circle back in here about sundown to bed."

"All right," Major de Spain said. "You boys take the horses. We'll go on out to the road in the wagon and wait there." He and General Compson and McCaslin got into the wagon and Boon and Walter and Sam and the boy mounted the horses and turned back and out of the trail. Sam led them for an hour through the gray and unmarked afternoon whose light was little different from what it had been at dawn and which would become darkness without any graduation between. Then Sam stopped them.

"This is far enough," he said. "He'll be coming upwind, and he don't want to smell the mules." They tied the mounts in a thicket. Sam led them on foot now, unpathed through the markless afternoon, the boy pressing close behind him, the two others, or so it seemed to the boy, on his heels. But they were not. Twice Sam turned his head slightly and spoke back to him across his shoulder, still walking: "You got time. We'll get there 'fore he does."

So he tried to go slower. He tried deliberately to decelerate the dizzy rushing of time in which the buck which he had not even seen was moving, which it seemed to him must be carrying the buck farther and farther and more and more irretrievably away from them even though there were no dogs behind him now to make him run, even though, according to Sam, he must have completed his circle now and was heading back toward them. They went on; it could have been another hour or twice that or less than half, the boy could not have said. Then they were on a ridge. He had never been in here before and he could not see that it was a ridge. He just knew that the earth had risen slightly because the underbrush had thinned a little, the ground sloping invisibly away toward a dense wall of cane. Sam stopped. "This is it," he said. He spoke to Walter and Boon: "Follow this ridge and you will come to two crossings. You will see the tracks. If he crosses, it will be at one of these three."

Walter looked about for a moment. "I know it," he said. "I've even seen your deer. I was in here last Monday. He ain't nothing but a yearling."

"A yearling?" Boon said. He was panting from the walking. His face still looked a little wild. "If the one I saw was any yearling, I'm still in kindergarten."

"Then I must have seen a rabbit," Walter said. "I always heard you quit school altogether two years before the first grade."

Boon glared at Walter. "If you don't want to shoot him, get out of the way," he said. "Set down somewhere. By God, I——"

"Ain't nobody going to shoot him standing here," Sam said quietly.

"Sam's right," Walter said. He moved, slanting the worn, silver-colored barrel of his rifle downward to walk with it again. "A little more moving and a little more quiet too. Five miles is still Hogganbeck range, even if we wasn't downwind." They went on. The boy could still hear Boon talking, though presently that ceased too. Then once more he and Sam stood motionless together against a tremendous pin oak in a little thicket, and again there was nothing. There was only the soaring and sombre solitude in the dim light, there was the thin murmur of the faint cold rain which had not ceased all day. Then, as if it had waited for them to find their positions and become still, the wilderness breathed again. It seemed to lean inward above them, above himself and Sam and Walter and Boon in their separate lurking-places, tremendous, attentive, impartial and omniscient, the buck moving in it somewhere, not running yet since he had not been pursued, not frightened yet and never fearsome but just alert also as they were alert, perhaps already circling back, perhaps quite near, perhaps conscious also of the eye of the ancient immortal Umpire. Because he was just twelve then, and that morning something had happened to him: in less than a second he had ceased forever to be the child he was yesterday. Or perhaps that made no difference, perhaps even a city-bred man, let alone a child, could not have understood it; perhaps only a country-bred one could comprehend loving the life he spills. He began to shake again.

"I'm glad it's started now," he whispered. He did not

move to speak; only his lips shaped the expiring words: "Then it will be gone when I raise the gun——"

Nor did Sam. "Hush," he said.

"Is he that near?" the boy whispered. "Do you think——"

"Hush," Sam said. So he hushed. But he could not stop the shaking. He did not try, because he knew it would go away when he needed the steadiness—had not Sam Fathers already consecrated and absolved him from weakness and regret too?—not from love and pity for all which lived and ran and then ceased to live in a second in the very midst of splendor and speed, but from weakness and regret. So they stood motionless, breathing deep and quiet and steady. If there had been any sun, it would be near to setting now; there was a condensing, a densifying, of what he had thought was the gray and unchanging light until he realised suddenly that it was his own breathing, his heart, his blood —something, all things, and that Sam Fathers had marked him indeed, not as a mere hunter, but with something Sam had had in his turn of his vanished and forgotten people. He stopped breathing then; there was only his heart, his blood, and in the following silence the wilderness ceased to breathe also, leaning, stooping overhead with its breath held, tremendous and impartial and waiting. Then the shaking stopped too, as he had known it would, and he drew back the two heavy hammers of the gun.

Then it had passed. It was over. The solitude did not breathe again yet; it had merely stopped watching him and was looking somewhere else, even turning its back on him,

looking on away up the ridge at another point, and the boy
knew as well as if he had seen him that the buck had come
to the edge of the cane and had either seen or scented them
and faded back into it. But the solitude did not breathe
again. It should have suspired again then but it did not. It
was still facing, watching, what it had been watching and it
was not here, not where he and Sam stood; rigid, not breathing himself, he thought, cried *No! No!*, knowing already
that it was too late, thinking with the old despair of two and
three years ago: *I'll never get a shot.* Then he heard it—the
flat single clap of Walter Ewell's rifle which never missed.
Then the mellow sound of the horn came down the ridge
and something went out of him and he knew then he had
never expected to get the shot at all.

"I reckon that's it," he said. "Walter got him." He had
raised the gun slightly without knowing it. He lowered it
again and had lowered one of the hammers and was already
moving out of the thicket when Sam spoke.

"Wait."

"Wait?" the boy cried. And he would remember that—
how he turned upon Sam in the truculence of a boy's grief
over the missed opportunity, the missed luck. "What for?
Don't you hear that horn?"

And he would remember how Sam was standing. Sam
had not moved. He was not tall, squat rather and broad, and
the boy had been growing fast for the past year or so and
there was not much difference between them in height, yet
Sam was looking over the boy's head and up the ridge
toward the sound of the horn and the boy knew that Sam

did not even see him; that Sam knew he was still there beside him but he did not see the boy. Then the boy saw the
buck. It was coming down the ridge, as if it were walking
out of the very sound of the horn which related its death.
It was not running, it was walking, tremendous, unhurried,
slanting and tilting its head to pass the antlers through the
undergrowth, and the boy standing with Sam beside him
now instead of behind him as Sam always stood, and the gun
still partly aimed and one of the hammers still cocked.

Then it saw them. And still it did not begin to run. It
just stopped for an instant, taller than any man, looking at
them; then its muscles suppled, gathered. It did not even
alter its course, not fleeing, not even running, just moving
with that winged and effortless ease with which deer move,
passing within twenty feet of them, its head high and the
eye not proud and not haughty but just full and wild and
unafraid, and Sam standing beside the boy now, his right
arm raised at full length, palm-outward, speaking in that
tongue which the boy had learned from listening to him
and Joe Baker in the blacksmith shop, while up the ridge
Walter Ewell's horn was still blowing them into a dead
buck.

"Oleh, Chief," Sam said. "Grandfather."

When they reached Walter, he was standing with his
back toward them, quite still, bemused almost, looking
down at his feet. He didn't look up at all.

"Come here, Sam," he said quietly. When they reached
him he still did not look up, standing above a little spike
buck which had still been a fawn last spring. "He was so

little I pretty near let him go," Walter said. "But just look at the track he was making. It's pretty near big as a cow's. If there were any more tracks here besides the ones he is laying in, I would swear there was another buck here that I never even saw."

3.   It was dark when they reached the road where the surrey waited. It was turning cold, the rain had stopped, and the sky was beginning to blow clear. His cousin and Major de Spain and General Compson had a fire going. "Did you get him?" Major de Spain said.

"Got a good-sized swamp-rabbit with spike horns," Walter said. He slid the little buck down from his mule. The boy's cousin McCaslin looked at it.

"Nobody saw the big one?" he said.

"I don't even believe Boon saw it," Walter said. "He probably jumped somebody's straw cow in that thicket." Boon started cursing, swearing at Walter and at Sam for not getting the dogs in the first place and at the buck and all.

"Never mind," Major de Spain said. "He'll be here for us next fall. Let's get started home."

It was after midnight when they let Walter out at his gate two miles from Jefferson and later still when they took General Compson to his house and then returned to Major de Spain's, where he and McCaslin would spend the rest of the night, since it was still seventeen miles home. It was cold, the sky was clear now; there would be a heavy frost by sunup and the ground was already frozen beneath the horses' feet and the wheels and beneath their own feet as they crossed Major de Spain's yard and entered the house, the warm dark house, feeling their way up the dark stairs until Major de Spain found a candle and lit it, and into the strange room and the big deep bed, the still cold sheets until they began to warm to their bodies and at last the shaking stopped and suddenly he was telling McCaslin about it while McCaslin listened, quietly until he had finished. "You don't believe it," the boy said. "I know you don't——"

"Why not?" McCaslin said. "Think of all that has happened here, on this earth. All the blood hot and strong for living, pleasuring, that has soaked back into it. For grieving and suffering too, of course, but still getting something out of it for all that, getting a lot out of it, because after all you don't have to continue to bear what you believe is suffering; you can always choose to stop that, put an end to that. And even suffering and grieving is better than nothing; there is only one thing worse than not being alive, and that's shame. But you can't be alive forever, and you always wear out life long before you have exhausted the possibilities of living. And all that must be somewhere; all that could not have been invented and created just to be thrown away. And the earth is shallow; there is not a great deal of it before you come to the rock. And the earth don't want to just keep things, hoard them; it wants to use them again. Look at the seed, the acorns, at what happens even to carrion when you try to bury it: it refuses too, seethes and struggles too until it reaches light and air again, hunting the sun still. And they —" the boy saw his hand in silhouette for a moment against the window beyond which, accustomed to the darkness now, he could see sky where the scoured and icy stars glittered "—they don't want it, need it. Besides, what would it want, itself, knocking around out there, when it never had enough time about the earth as it was, when there is plenty of room about the earth, plenty of places still unchanged from what they were when the blood used and pleasured in them while it was still blood?"

"But we want them," the boy said. "We want them too. There is plenty of room for us and them too."

"That's right," McCaslin said. "Suppose they don't have substance, can't cast a shadow——"

"But I saw it!" the boy cried. "I saw him!"

"Steady," McCaslin said. For an instant his hand touched the boy's flank beneath the covers. "Steady. I know you did. So did I. Sam took me in there once after I killed my first deer."

This is how Herman Basket told it:

In the old days, the steamboat came all the way up the River, right to the Plantation. In the winter, when the water was high, it swam almost to the door of the House, though sometimes in the spring, as the water went down, it would have to walk a little now and then. Then one summer it waited too long and this time it could not even walk back to Vicksburg. So it crawled up on a sand-bar and died and the white men who owned it removed the swimming machinery and carried it back to Vicksburg and now the steamboat belonged to anyone who wanted it, assuming anyone was that foolish.

Or so the People thought then, right up to the very moment in fact when one day the House became too small for all who wished to sleep inside and almost before the People could complain, the Man said, "Tomorrow we will fetch the steamboat." That sand-bar was twelve miles away and that steamboat was almost as large as the House so the next morning there was no one in the Plantation except the Man and the black people. It took the Man all that day to find the People. He used the dogs; he found some of the People in hollow logs in the bottom. That night he made all the men sleep in the House. He kept the dogs in the House too. So the next morning all the men were able to go to the steamboat.

Every night the Man would make all the men sleep in the House, with the dogs in the house too, and each morning they would return to the steamboat. They would go in the wagons, since the Man did not wish them to be so tired from the twelve-mile walk that they would not pull strongly on the ropes. Though he would not let them ride in the wagons back to the Plantation at night because he wished the mules to be fresh also for tomorrow.

Finally the steamboat was out of the river bottom. It had taken five months to get it out of the bottom, because they had to cut down the trees to make a path for it. But now it could walk faster on the logs, with all the men pulling on the ropes and the Man sitting in his chair on the front gallery of the boat, with one boy to hold over him the purple parasol which the white New Orleans trader calling himself the Chevalier Soeur-Blonde de Vitry said came from Paris beyond the Stinking Water, and

*another boy with a branch to drive away the flying beasts.
The dogs rode on the boat too and sometimes the Man
would wear the red slippers too though after only an
hour even he would begin to sweat. Then after another
hour he would take them off and sit in his bare feet
looking down at the People and the black men pulling the
ropes which made the steamboat walk.*

*Then it was winter. The Man did not need the parasol
now and the flying beasts had departed also; now both
of the boys could tend the fire in the chimney which the
Man had caused to be built on the front gallery of the
steamboat so that now even on the coldest days the Man
could sit comfortably in his chair before the hearth and
watch the People and the black men drawing on the ropes
which made the steamboat walk.*

*Then at last the steamboat reached the Plantation,
where it could die again. Or so the People thought.
Indeed, the Man always said afterward that he had a
great deal more trouble arranging with the People to
move it that last few feet to the House than he had with
all the twelve miles from the sand-bar. But at last the
steamboat was beside the House to suit him, and now the
People could sit down again and go about their own
affairs. (Until, that is, the Man thought of something else
arduous and unpleasant for them to do. Because Doom
had no sense of humor. He was always saying things like,
since the people wished him to be the Man, he*

supposed he would have to be the Man, and
that the only way he knew to be a king was to
be one.) Axes were used to chop through one side of the
House and through the side of the steamboat next to
it and now anyone who wished could go from the House
to the steamboat or vice versa without having to come
outdoors, and now there was room for all to sleep inside.
But (Herman Basket said) not he. As soon as he lay
down inside the House or the steamboat either, he would
become so nervous just remembering how tired the
steamboat had used to make him that he would have to
rise and take up his blanket and go outside and find a
thicket so dense and distant that he couldn't see either
one of them. Only then could he compose himself for
sleep.

3

A BEAR
HUNT

RATLIFF IS TELLING THIS. He is a sewing-machine agent; time was when he traveled about our county in a light, strong buckboard drawn by a sturdy, wiry, mismatched team of horses; now he uses a model T Ford, which also carries his demonstrator machine in a tin box on the rear, shaped like a dog kennel and painted to resemble a house.

Ratliff may be seen anywhere without surprise—the only man present at the bazaars and sewing bees of farmers' wives; moving among both men and women at all-day singings at country churches, and singing, too, in a pleasant baritone. He was even at this bear hunt of which he speaks, at the annual hunting camp of Major de Spain in the river bottom twenty miles from town, even though there was no one there to whom he might possibly have sold a machine, since Mrs. de Spain doubtless already owned one, unless she had given it to one of her married daughters, and the other man—Lucius Hogganbeck—with whom he became involved, to the violent detriment of his face and other members, could not have bought one for his wife even if he would, without Ratliff sold it to him on indefinite credit.

Lucius Hogganbeck was one of the children of that Boon Hogganbeck who had been the utterly loyal and completely unreliable man-Friday of old Major de Spain and Mr. McCaslin Edmonds back in the time when they and Uncle Isaac McCaslin and Walter Ewell and old General Compson who was my grandfather (and old Ash Wylie too, the father of this Ash who figured in Ratliff's affair, and of whom only Uncle Ike remains) were the hunting club. But

Lucius is forty now and most of his teeth are gone, and it is years now since he and two brothers named Provine were known in Jefferson as the Provine gang and terrorized our quiet town after the unimaginative fashion of wild youth by letting off pistols on the square late Saturday nights or galloping their horses down scurrying and screaming lanes of churchgoing ladies on Sunday morning. Younger citizens of the town do not know him at all save as a tall, apparently strong and healthy man who loafs in a brooding, saturnine fashion wherever he will be allowed, never exactly accepted by any group, and who makes no effort whatever to support his wife and three children.

There are other men among us now whose families are in want; men who, perhaps, would not work anyway, but who now, since the last few years, cannot find work. These all attain and hold to a certain respectability by acting as agents for the manufacturers of minor articles like soap and men's toilet accessories and kitchen objects, being seen constantly about the square and the streets carrying small black sample cases. One day, to our surprise, Hogganbeck also appeared with such a case, though within less than a week the town officers discovered that it contained whisky in pint bottles. Major de Spain (not the old one: he was dead. This was his son, a banker, called Major in memory of his father and the rank and title which his father had earned and bore valiantly by 1865) extricated him somehow, as it was Major de Spain who supported his family by eking out the money which Mrs. Hogganbeck earned by sewing and such—bearing the burden of Lucius for the same reason as the gallant one of his father's military title: because old Major de Spain (along with Mr. Edmonds) had supported Boon all his life; or perhaps, we liked to believe, as a Roman gesture of salute and farewell to the bright figure which Lucius had been before time whipped him.

For there are older men who remember the Butch—he has even lost somewhere in his shabby past the lusty dare-devil-try of the nickname—Lucius of twenty years ago; that youth without humor, yet with some driving, inarticulate zest for breathing which has long since burned out of him, who performed in a fine frenzy, which was, perhaps, mostly alcohol, certain outrageous and spontaneous deeds, one of which was the Negro-picnic business. The picnic was at a Negro church a few miles from town. In the midst of it, Lucius and the two Provines, returning from a dance in the country, rode up with drawn pistols and freshly lit cigars; and taking the Negro men one by one, held the burning cigar ends to the popular celluloid collars of the day, leaving each victim's neck ringed with an abrupt and faint and pain-less ring of carbon. This is he of whom Ratliff is talking.

But there is one thing more which must be told here in order to set the stage for Ratliff. Five miles farther down the river from Major de Spain's camp, and in an even wilder part of the river's jungle of cane and gum and pin oak, there is an Indian mound. Aboriginal, it rises profoundly and darkly enigmatic, the only elevation of any kind in the wild, flat jungle of river bottom. Even to some of us—children though we were, yet we were descended of literate, town-bred people—it possessed inferences of secret and violent blood, of savage and sudden destruction, as though the yells and hatchets which we associated with Indians through the hidden and secret dime novels which we passed among ourselves were but trivial and momentary manifestations of what dark power still dwelled or lurked there, sinister, a little sardonic, like a dark and nameless beast lightly and lazily slumbering with boody jaws—this, perhaps, due to the fact that a remnant of a once powerful clan of the Chickasaw tribe still lived beside it under Government protection. They now had American names and they lived as the sparse white people who surrounded them in turn lived.

Yet we never saw them, since they never came to town, having their own settlement and store. When we grew older we realized that they were no wilder or more illiterate than the white people, and that probably their greatest deviation from the norm—and this, in our country, no especial deviation—was the fact that they were a little better than suspect to manufacture moonshine whisky back in the swamps. Yet to us, as children, they were a little fabulous, their swamp-hidden lives inextricable from the life of the dark mound, which some of us had never seen, yet of which we had all heard, as though they had been set by the dark powers to be guardians of it.

As I said, some of us had never seen the mound, yet all of us had heard of it, talked of it as boys will. It was as much a part of our lives and background as the land itself, as the lost Civil War and Sherman's march, or that there were Negroes among us living in economic competition who bore our family names; only more immediate, more potential and alive. When I was fifteen, a companion and I, on a dare, went into the mound one day just at sunset. We saw some of those Indians for the first time; we got directions from them and reached the top of the mound just as the sun set. We had camping equipment with us, but we made no fire. We didn't even make down our beds. We just sat side by side on that mound until it became light enough to find our way back to the road. We didn't talk. When we looked at each other in the gray dawn, our faces were gray, too, quiet, very grave. When we reached town again, we didn't talk either. We just parted and went home and went to bed. That's what we thought, felt, about the mound. We were children, it is true, yet we were descendants of people who read books and who were—or should have been—beyond superstition and impervious to mindless fear.

Now Ratliff tells about Lucius Hogganbeck and his hiccup.

When I got back to town, the first fellow I met says, "What happened to your face, Ratliff? Was De Spain using you in place of his bear hounds?"

"No, boys," I says. "Hit was a cattymount."

"What was you trying to do to hit, Ratliff?" a fellow says.

"Boys," I says, "be dog if I know."

And that was the truth. Hit was a good while after they had done hauled Luke Hogganbeck offen me that I found that out. Because I never knowed who Old Man Ash was, no more than Luke did. I just knowed that he was Major's nigger, a-helping around camp. All I knowed, when the

whole thing started, was what I thought I was aiming to do
—to maybe help Luke sho enough, or maybe at the outside
to just have a little fun with him without hurting him, or
even maybe to do Major a little favor by getting Luke
outen camp for a while. And then hyer hit is about midnight and that durn fellow comes swurging outen the woods
wild as a skeered deer, and runs in where they are setting
at the poker game, and I says, "Well, you ought to be satisfied. You done run clean out from under them." And he
stopped dead still and give me a kind of glare of wild astonishment; he didn't even know that they had quit; and then
he swurged all over me like a barn falling down.

Hit sho stopped that poker game. Hit taken three or four
of them to drag him offen me, with Major turned in his
chair with a set of threes in his hand, a-hammering on the
table and hollering cusses. Only a right smart of the helping
they done was stepping on my face and hands and feet. Hit
was like a fahr—the fellows with the water hose done the
most part of the damage.

"What the tarnation hell does this mean?" Major hollers,
with three or four fellows holding Luke, and him crying
like a baby.

"He set them on me!" Luke says. "He was the one sent
me up there, and I'm a-going to kill him!"

"Set who on you?" Major says.

"Them Indians!" Luke says, crying. Then he tried to get
at me again, flinging them fellows holding his arms around
like they was rag dolls, until Major pure cussed him quiet.
He's a man yet. Don't let hit fool you none because he

claims he ain't strong enough to work. Maybe hit's because he ain't never wore his strength down toting around one of them little black satchels full of pink galluses and shaving soap. Then Major asked me what hit was all about, and I told him how I had just been trying to help Luke get shed of them hiccups.

Be dog if I didn't feel right sorry for him. I happened to be passing out that way, and so I just thought I would drop in on them and see what luck they was having, and I druv up about sundown, and the first fellow I see was Luke. I wasn't surprised, since this here would be the biggest present gathering of men in the county, let alone the free eating and whisky, so I says, "Well, this is a surprise." And he says:

"Hic-uh! Hic-ow! Hic-oh! Hic—oh, God!" He had done already had them since nine o'clock the night before; he had been teching the jug ever' time Major offered him one and ever' time he could get to hit when Old Man Ash wasn't looking; and two days before Major had killed a bear, and I reckon Luke had already et more possum-rich bear pork—let alone the venison they had, with maybe a few coons and squirls throwed in for seasoning—than he could have hauled off in a waggin. So here he was, going three times to the minute, like one of these here clock bombs; only hit was bear meat and whisky instead of dynamite, and so he couldn't explode and put himself outen his misery.

They told me how he had done already kept ever'body awake most of the night before, and how Major got up mad anyway, and went off with his gun and Ash to handle them two bear hounds, and Luke following—outen pure misery, I reckon, since he hadn't slept no more than nobody else— walking along behind Major, saying, "Hic-ah! Hic-ow! Hic-oh! Hic—oh, Lord!" until Major turns on him and says:

"Get to hell over yonder with them shotgun fellows on the deer stands. How do you expect me to walk up on a bear or even hear the dogs when they strike? I might as well be riding a motorcycle."

So Luke went on back to where the deer standers was along the log-line levee. I reckon he never so much went away as he kind of died away in the distance like that ere motorcycle Major mentioned. He never tried to be quiet. I reckon he knowed hit wouldn't be no use. He never tried to keep to the open, neither. I reckon he thought that any fool would know from his sound that he wasn't no deer. No. I reckon he was so mizzable by then that he hoped somebody would shoot him. But nobody never, and he come to the first stand, where Uncle Ike McCaslin was, and set down on a log behind Uncle Ike with his elbows on his knees and his face in his hands, going, "Hic-uh! Hic-uh! Hic-uh! Hic-uh!" until Uncle Ike turns and says:

"Confound you, boy; get away from here. Do you reckon any varmint in the world is going to walk up to a hay baler? Go drink some water."

"I done already done that," Luke says, without moving. "I been drinking water since nine o'clock last night. I done already drunk so much water that if I was to fall down I would gush like a artesian well."

"Well, go away anyhow," Uncle Ike says. "Get away from here."

So Luke gets up and kind of staggers away again, kind of dying away again like he was run by one of these hyer one-cylinder gasoline engines, only a durn sight more often and regular. He went on down the levee to where the next stand was, and they druv him way from there, and he went on toward the next one. I reckon he was still hoping that some-body would take pity on him and shoot him, because now he kind of seemed to give up. Now, when he come to the "oh, God" part of hit, they said you could hyear him clean back to camp. They said he would echo back from the cane-brake across the river like one of these hyer loud-speakers down in a well. They said that even the dogs on the trail quit baying, and so they all come up and made him come back to camp. That's where he was when I come in. And Old Man Ash was there, too, where him and Major had done come in so Major could take a nap, and neither me nor Luke noticing him except as just another nigger around.

That was hit. Neither one of us knowed or even thought about him. I be dog if hit don't look like sometimes that when a fellow sets out to play a joke, hit ain't another fellow he's playing that joke on; hit's a kind of big power laying still somewhere in the dark that he sets out to prank with without knowing hit, and hit all depends on whether that ere power is in the notion to take a joke or not, whether or not hit blows up right in his face like this one did in mine. Because I says, "You done had them since nine o'clock yes-terday? That's nigh twenty-four hours. Seems like to me you'd 'a' done something to try to stop them." And him looking at me like he couldn't make up his mind whether to jump up and bite my head off or just to try and bite hisn off, saying "Hic-uh! Hic-uh!" slow and regular. Then he says,

"I don't want to get shed of them. I like them. But if you had them, I would get shed of them for you. You want to know how?"

"How?" I says.

"I'd just tear your head off. Then you wouldn't have nothing to hiccup with. They wouldn't worry you then. I'd be glad to do hit for you."

"Sho now," I says, looking at him setting there on the kitchen steps—hit was after supper, but he hadn't et none, being as his throat had done turned into a one-way street on him, you might say—going "Hic-uh! Hic-oh! Hic-oh! Hic-uh!" because I reckon Major had done told him what would happen to him if he taken to hollering again. I never meant no harm. Besides, they had done already told me how he had kept everybody awake all night the night before and had done skeered all the game outen that part of the bottom, and besides, the walk might help him to pass his own time. So I says, "I believe I know how you might get shed of them. But, of course, if you don't want to get shed of them——"

And he says, "I just wish somebody would tell me how. I'd pay ten dollars just to set here for one minute without saying 'hic' ——" Well, that set him off sho enough. Hit was like up to that time his insides had been satisfied with going "hic-uh" steady, but quiet, but now, when he reminded himself, hit was like he had done opened a cut-out, because right away he begun hollering, "Hic—oh, God!" like when them fellows on the deer stands had made him come back to camp, and I heard Major's feet coming bup-bup-bup across the floor. Even his feet sounded mad, and I says quick,

"Sh-h-h-h! You don't want to get Major mad again, now."

So he quieted some, setting there on the kitchen steps, with Old Man Ash and the other niggers moving around inside the kitchen, and he says, "I will try anything you can sujest. I done tried ever'thing I knowed and ever'thing anybody else told me to. I done held my breath and drunk water until I feel just like one of these hyer big automobile tahrs they use to advertise with, and I hung by my knees offen that limb yonder for fifteen minutes and drunk a pint bottle full of water upside down, and somebody said to swallow a buckshot and I done that. And still I got them. What do you know that I can do?"

"Well," I says, "I don't know what you would do. But if hit was me that had them, I'd go up to the mound and get old John Basket to cure me."

Then he set right still, and then he turned slow and looked at me; I be dog if for a minute he didn't even hiccup. "John Basket?" he says.

"Sho," I says. "Them Indians knows all sorts of dodges that white doctors ain't hyeard about yet. He'd be glad to do that much for a white man, too, them pore aboriginees would, because the white folks have been so good to them— not only letting them keep that ere hump of dirt that don't nobody want noways, but letting them use names like ourn and selling them flour and sugar and farm tools at not no more than a fair profit above what they would cost a white man. I hyear tell how pretty soon they are even going to start letting them come to town once a week. Old Basket would be glad to cure them hiccups for you."

"John Basket," he says; "them Indians," he says, hiccuping slow and quiet and steady. Then he says right sudden, "I be dog if I will!" Then I be dog if hit didn't sound like he was crying. He jumped up and stood there cussing, sounding like he was crying. "Hit ain't a man hyer has got any mercy on me, white or black. Hyer I done suffered and suffered more than twenty-four hours without food or sleep, and not a sonabitch of them has any mercy or pity on me!"

"Well, I was trying to," I says. "Hit ain't me that's got them. I just thought, seeing as how you had done seemed to got to the place where couldn't no white man help you. But hit ain't no law making you go up there and get shed of them." So I made like I was going away. I went back around the corner of the kitchen and watched him set down on the steps again, going "Hic-uh! Hic-uh!" slow and quiet again; and then I seen, through the kitchen window, Old Man Ash standing just inside the kitchen door, right still, with his head bent like he was listening. But still I never suspected nothing. Not even did I suspect nothing when, after a while, I watched Luke get up again, sudden but quiet, and stand for a minute looking at the window where the poker game and the folks was, and then look off into the dark towards the road that went down the bottom. Then he went into

the house, quiet, and come out a minute later with a lighted
lantrun and a shotgun. I don't know whose gun hit was and
I don't reckon he did, nor cared neither. He just come out
kind of quiet and determined, and went on down the road.
I could see the lantrun, but I could hyear him a long time
after the lantrun had done disappeared. I had come back
around the kitchen then and I was listening to him dying
away down the bottom, when old Ash says behind me:

"He gwine up dar?"

"Up where?" I says.

"Up to de mound," he says.

"Why, I be dog if I know," I says. "The last time I talked
to him he never sounded like he was fixing to go nowhere.
Maybe he just decided to take a walk. Hit might do him
some good; make him sleep tonight and help him get up a
appetite for breakfast maybe. What do you think?"

But Ash never said nothing. He just went on back into the
kitchen. And still I never suspected nothing. How could I?
I hadn't never even seen Jefferson in them days. I hadn't
never even seen a pair of shoes, let alone two stores in a row
or a arc light.

So I went on in where the poker game was, and I says,
"Well, gentlemen, I reckon we might get some sleep tonight." And I told them what had happened, because more
than like he would stay up there until daylight rather than
walk them five miles back in the dark, because maybe them
Indians wouldn't mind a little thing like a fellow with hiccups, like white folks would. And I be dog if Major didn't
rear up about hit.

"Dammit, Ratliff," he says, "you ought not to done that."

"Why, I just sujested hit to him, Major, for a joke," I says. "I just told him about how old Basket was a kind of doctor. I never expected him to take hit serious. Maybe he ain't even going up there. Maybe's he's just went out after a coon."

But most of them felt about hit like I did. "Let him go," Mr. Fraser says. "I hope he walks around all night. Damn if I slept a wink for him all night long. . . . Deal the cards, Uncle Ike."

"Can't stop him now, noways," Uncle Ike says, dealing the cards. "And maybe John Basket can do something for his hiccups. Durn young fool, eating and drinking himself to where he can't talk nor swallow neither. He set behind me on a log this morning, sounding just like a hay baler. I thought once I'd have to shoot him to get rid of him. . . . Queen bets a quarter, gentlemen."

So I set there watching them, thinking now and then about that durn fellow with his shotgun and his lantrun stumbling and blundering along through the woods, walking five miles in the dark to get shed of his hiccups, with the varmints all watching him and wondering just what kind of a hunt this was and just what kind of a two-leg varmint hit was that made a noise like that, and about them Indians up at the mound when he would come walking in, and I would have to laugh until Major says, "What in hell are you mumbling and giggling at?"

"Nothing," I says. "I was just thinking about a fellow I know."

"And damn if you hadn't ought to be out there with

him," Major says. Then he decided hit was about drink time and he begun to holler for Ash. Finally I went to the door and hollered for Ash towards the kitchen, but hit was another one of the niggers that answered. When he come in with the demijohn and fixings, Major looks up and says "Where's Ash?"

"He done gone," the nigger says.

"Gone?" Major says. "Gone where?"

"He say he gwine up to'ds de mound," the nigger says. And still I never knowed, never suspected. I just thought to myself, "That old nigger has turned powerful tender-hearted all of a sudden, being skeered for Luke Hoggan-beck to walk around by himself in the dark. Or maybe Ash likes to listen to them hiccups," I thought to myself.

"Up to the mound?" Major says. "By dad, if he comes back here full of John Basket's bust-skull whisky I'll skin him alive."

"He ain't say what he gwine fer," the nigger says. "All he tell me when he left, he gwine up to'ds de mound and he be back by daylight."

"He better be," Major says. "He better be sober too."

So we set there and they went on playing and me watch-ing them like a durn fool, not suspecting nothing, just thinking how hit was a shame that that durned old nigger would have to come in and spoil Luke's trip, and hit come along towards eleven o'clock and they begun to talk about going to bed, being as they was all going out on stand to-morrow, when we hyeard the sound. Hit sounded like a drove of wild horses coming up that road, and we hadn't no more than turned towards the door, a-asking one another what in tarnation hit could be, with Major just saying, "What in the name of——" when hit come across the porch like a harrycane and down the hall, and the door busted open and there Luke was. He never had no gun and lantrun then, and his clothes was nigh tore clean offen him, and his face looked wild as ere a man in the Jackson a-sylum. But the main thing I noticed was that he wasn't hiccuping now. And this time, too, he was nigh crying.

"They was fixing to kill me!" he says. "They was going to burn me to death! They had done tried me and tied me onto the pile of wood, and one of them was coming with the fahr when I managed to bust loose and run!"

"Who was?" Major says. "What in the tarnation hell are you talking about?"

"Them Indians!" Luke says. "They was fixing to——"

"What?" Major hollers. "Damn to blue blazes, what?"

And that was where I had to put my foot in hit. He hadn't never seen me until then. "At least they cured your hiccups," I says.

Hit was then that he stopped right still. He hadn't never even seen me, but he seen me now. He stopped right still and looked at me with that ere wild face that looked like hit had just escaped from Jackson and had ought to be took back there quick.

"What?" he says.

"Anyway, you done run out from under them hiccups," I says.

Well, sir, he stood there for a full minute. His eyes had

done gone blank, and he stood there with his head cocked a little, listening to his own insides. I reckon hit was the first time he had took time to find out that they was gone. He stood there right still for a full minute while that ere kind of shocked astonishment come onto his face. Then he jumped on me. I was still setting in my chair, and I be dog if for a minute I didn't think the roof had done fell in.

Well, they got him offen me at last and got him quieted down, and then they washed me off and give me a drink, and I felt better. But even with that drink I never felt so good but what I felt hit was my duty to my honor to call him outen the back yard, as the fellow says. No, sir. I know when I done made a mistake and guessed wrong; Major de Spain wasn't the only man that caught a bear on that hunt; no, sir. I be dog, if it had been daylight, I'd a hitched up my Ford and taken out of there. But hit was midnight, and besides, that nigger, Ash, was on my mind then. I had just begun to suspect that hit was more to this business than met the nekkid eye. And hit wasn't no good time then to go back to the kitchen then and ask him about hit, because Luke was using the kitchen. Major had give him a drink, too, and he was back there, making up for them two days he hadn't et, talking a right smart about what he aimed to do to such and such a sonabitch that would try to play his durn jokes on him, not mentioning no names; but mostly laying himself in a new set of hiccups, though I ain't going back to see.

So I waited until daylight, until I hyeard the niggers stirring around in the kitchen; then I went back there. And there was old Ash, looking like he always did, oiling Major's boots and setting them behind the stove and then taking up Major's rifle and beginning to load the magazine. He just looked once at my face when I come in, and went on shoving ca'tridges into the gun.

"So you went up to the mound last night," I says. He looked up at me again, quick, and then down again. But he never said nothing, looking like a durned old frizzle-headed ape. "You must know some of them folks up there," I says.

"I knows some of um," he says, shoving ca'tridges into the gun.

"You know old John Basket?" I says.

"I knows some of um," he says, not looking at me.

"Did you see him last night?" I says. He never said nothing at all. So then I changed my tone, like a fellow has to do to get anything outen a nigger. "Look here," I says. "Look at me." He looked at me. "Just what did you do up there last night?"

"Who, me?" he says.

"Come on," I says. "Hit's all over now. Mr. Hogganbeck has done got over his hiccups and we done both forgot about anything that might have happened when he got back last night. You never went up there just for fun last night. Or maybe hit was something you told them up there, told old man Basket. Was that hit?" He had done quit looking at me, but he never stopped shoving ca'tridges into that gun. He looked quick to both sides. "Come on," I says. "Do you want to tell me what happened up there, or do you want me to mention to Mr. Hogganbeck that you was mixed up in hit some way?" He never stopped loading the rifle and he never looked at me, but I be dog if I couldn't almost see his mind working. "Come on," I says. "Just what was you doing up there last night?"

Then he told me. I reckon he knowed hit wasn't no use to try to hide hit then; that if I never told Luke, I could still tell Major. "I jest dodged him and got dar first en told um he was a new revenue agent coming up dar tonight, but dat he warn't much en dat all dey had to do was to give um a good skeer en likely he would go away. En dey did en he did."

"Well!" I says. "Well! I always thought I was pretty good at joking folks," I says, "but I take a back seat for you. What happened?" I says. "Did you see hit?"

"Never much happened," he says. "Dey jest went down de road a piece en atter a while hyer he come a-hicken' en a-blumpin' up de road wid de lant'un en de gun. They took de lant'un en de gun away frum him en took him up pon topper de mound en talked de Injun language at him fer a while. Den dey piled up some wood en fixed him on hit so he could git loose in a minute, en den one of dem come up de hill wid de fire, en he done de rest."

"Well!" I says. "Well, I'll be eternally durned!" And then all on a sudden hit struck me. I had done turned and was going out when hit struck me, and I stopped and I says, "There's one more thing I want to know. Why did you do hit?"

Now he set there on the wood box, rubbing the gun with

his hand, not looking at me again. "I wuz jest helping you kyo him of dem hiccups."

"Come on," I says. "That wasn't your reason. What was hit? Remember, I got a right smart I can tell Mr. Hogganbeck and Major both now. I don't know what Major will do, but I know what Mr. Hogganbeck will do if I was to tell him."

And he set there, rubbing that ere rifle with his hand. He was kind of looking down, like he was thinking. Not like he was trying to decide whether to tell me or not, but like he was remembering something from a long time back. And that's exactly what he was doing, because he says:

"I ain't skeered for him to know. One time dey was a picnic. Hit was a long time back, nigh twenty years ago. He was a young man den, en in de middle of de picnic, him en two udder white men—I fergit dey name—rid up wid dey pistols out en cotch us niggers one at a time en burned our collars off. Hit was him dat burnt mine."

"And you waited all this time and went to all this trouble, just to get even with him?" I says.

"Hit warn't dat," he says, rubbing the rifle with his hand. "Hit wuz de collar. Back in dem days a top nigger hand made two dollars a week. I paid half of it fer dat collar. Hit wuz blue, wid a red picture of de race betwixt de Natchez en de Robert E. Lee running around hit. He burnt hit up. I makes ten dollars a week now. En I jest wish I knowed where I could buy another collar like dat un fer half of hit. I wish I did."

There were railroads in the wilderness now; people who used to go overland by carriage or horseback to the River landings for the Memphis and New Orleans steamboats could take the train from almost anywhere now. And presently Pullmans too, all the way from Chicago and the Northern cities and the Northern money, the Yankee dollars arriving between sheets and even in drawing rooms to open the wilderness, nudge it further and further toward obsolescence with the whine of saws; what had been one vast unbroken virgin span was now booming with cotton and timber both. Or rather, booming with simple money: increment's troglodyte which had fathered twin ones: solvency and bankruptcy, the three of them booming money into the land so fast now that the problem was to get rid of it before it whelmed you into strangulation.

*And now paved roads too as the cotton seed and the
lumber mills pushed what remained of the big woods
further and further southward into the V of the River and
the hills; when old Isaac McCaslin was a boy he shot
bear and deer and wild turkey after less than a day in a
mule-drawn wagon; even when he had got old enough for
young men to begin to call him Uncle Ike and the
distance was fifty miles instead of twenty, it still took
only a part of a day in the automobile, even though the
roads were dirt ones. Now they had concrete: a hundred
miles instead of fifty, then two hundred instead of one
as the wilderness dwindled southward into the notch of
the hills and the Old Man.*

*Sometimes it would seem to him that the three of them
—himself, the old hunter, and the hills and the vast
River—had presided over a cycle; or rather, not a cycle
but a mad and pointless merry-go-round, with two of
them anyway—the inviolable hills and the great invincible
almost inattentive River—impervious to it: the timber
which had to be logged and sold in order to deforest the
land in order to convert the soil to raising cotton in order
to sell the cotton in order to make the land valuable
enough to be worth spending money raising dykes to
keep the River off of it. Or try to, since the Old Man
didn't care about cotton, didn't give a damn about cotton
in fact; the Old Man and all his little contributing streams
levee'd too, himself paying none of the dykes any heed*

whatever when it suited his mood and fancy, gathering
water all the way from Montana to Pennsylvania every
generation or so and rolling it down the artificial gut of
his victims' puny and baseless hoping, piling the water
up, not fast, just inexorably, giving plenty of time to
measure his crest and telegraph ahead, even warning of
the exact day almost when he would enter the house and
float the piano out of it and the pictures off the walls, and
even remove the house itself if it were not securely
fastened down.

Inexorable and unhurried, overpassing one by one his
little confluent feeders and shoving the water into them
until for days their current would flow backward,
upstream: as far upstream as Wylie's Crossing where the
original, the authentic Major de Spain had established
the camp where he, the old hunter, had fifty years ago
made his esquire's vigil to the Big Woods and been
accepted, accoladed. The little rivers were dyked too, but
back here was the land of individualists: remnants and
descendants of the tall men now taken to farming, and of
Snopeses who were more than individualists: they were
Snopeses, so that where the owners of the thousand-acre
plantations along the Big River confederated as one man
with sandbags and machines and their Negro tenants
and wage-hands to hold the sandboils and the cracks,
back here the owner of the hundred- or two-hundred-acre
farm patrolled his section of levee with a sandbag in one

hand and his shotgun in the other, lest his upstream neighbor dynamite it to save his (the upstream neighbor's) own.

Piling up the water while white man and Negro worked side by side in shifts in the mud and the rain, with automobile headlights and gasoline flares and kegs of whisky and coffee boiling in fifty-gallon batches in scoured and scalded oil drums; lapping, tentative, almost innocently, merely inexorable (no hurry, his) among and beneath and between and finally over the frantic sandbags, as if his whole purpose had been merely to give man another chance to prove, not to him but to man, just how much the human body could bear, stand, endure; then, having let man prove it, doing what he could have done at any time these past weeks if so minded: removing with no haste, nor any particular malice or fury either, a mile or two miles of levee and coffee drums and whisky kegs and gas flares in one sloughing collapse, gleaming dully for a little while yet among the parallel cotton middles until the fields vanished along with the roads and lanes and at last the towns themselves.

Vanished, gone beneath one vast yellow motionless expanse, out of which projected only the tops of trees and telephone poles and the decapitations of human dwelling-places like enigmatic objects placed by inscrutable and impenetrable design on a dirty mirror;

*and the mounds of the predecessors on which, among a
tangle of moccasins, bear and horses and deer and mules
and wild turkeys and cows and domestic chickens waited
patient in mutual armistice; and the levees themselves,
where among a jumble of uxorious flotsam the young
continued to be born and the old to die, not from
exposure but from simple and normal time and decay,
as if man and his destiny were in the end stronger even
than the river which had dispossessed him, inviolable by
and invincible to alteration.*

*Then, having proved that too, he—the Old Man—
would withdraw, not retreat: subside, back from the land
slowly and inexorably too, emptying the confluent rivers
and bayous back into the old vain hopeful gut, but so
slowly and gradually that not the waters seemed to fall
but the flat earth itself to rise, creep in one plane back
into light and air again: one constant stain of
yellow-brown at one constant altitude on telephone poles
and the walls of gins and houses and stores as though
the line had been laid off with a transit and painted in
one gigantic unbroken brush stroke, the earth itself one
alluvial inch higher, the rich dirt one inch deeper, drying
into long cracks beneath the hot fierce glare of May:
but not for long, because almost at once came the plow,
the plowing and planting already two months late but
that did not matter: the cotton man-tall once more by
August and whiter and denser still by picking time, as if*

*the Old Man said, "I do what I want to, when I want to.
But I pay my way."*

*It was his native land; he had been born of it and his
bones would sleep in it—the cradling hills and the river
valley which they cradled—the hills along whose edge the
plantation lay where he had been born and where old
Sam Fathers, son of a Negro slave and a Chickasaw king,
had trained and taught him how to use a gun with care
and respect, in order to be worthy to enter the Big Woods
when his time came. The Big Woods, the Big Bottom,
the wilderness, vanished now from where he had first
known it; the very spot where he and Sam were standing
when he heard his first running hounds and cocked the
gun and saw the first buck, was now thirty feet below the
surface of a government-built flood-control reservoir
whose bottom was rising gradually and inexorably each
year on another layer of beer cans and bottle tops and
lost bass plugs; the wilderness itself, where he had served
his humble apprenticeship to the rough food and the
rough sleeping, the life of hungers: men and horses and
hounds, not to slay the game but to pursue it, touch and
let go, never satiety;—the wilderness, the Big Woods
themselves being shoved, pushed just as inexorably further
and further on until now the mile-long freight trains
were visible for miles across the cotton fields, seeming to
pass two or even three of the little Indian-named hamlets
at one time over the ground where every November they*

would run the ritual of the old warp-footed bear;—the
Big Woods, shoved, pushed further and further down into
the notch where the hills and the Big River met, where
they would make their last stand. It would be a good one
too, impregnable; by that time, they would be too dense,
too strong with life and memory, of all which had ever
run in them, ever to die—the strong irritable loud-reeking
bear, the gallant high-headed stags looking longer than
comets and pale as smoke, the music-ed and untiring
dogs and the splattered horses and the men who rode
them; himself too. Oh yes, he would think; me too. I've
been too busy all my life trying not to waste any living,
to have time left to die.

4

RACE
AT MORNING

I was in the boat when I seen him. It was jest dust-dark; I had jest fed the horses and clumb back down the bank to the boat and shoved off to cross back to camp when I seen him, about half a quarter up the river, swimming; jest his head above the water, and it no more than a dot in that light. But I could see that rocking chair he toted on it and I knowed it was him, going right back to that canebrake in the fork of the bayou where he lived all year until the day before the season opened, like the game wardens had give him a calendar, when he would clear out and disappear, nobody knowed where, until the day after the season closed. But here he was, coming back a day ahead of time, like maybe he had got mixed up and was using last year's calendar by mistake. Which was jest too bad for him, because me and Mister Ernest would be setting on the horse right over him when the sun rose tomorrow morning.

So I told Mister Ernest and we et supper and fed the dogs, and then I holp Mister Ernest in the poker game, standing behind his chair until about ten o'clock, when Roth Edmonds said, "Why don't you go to bed, boy?"

"Or if you're going to set up," Willy Legate said, "why don't you take a spelling book to set up over? He knows every cuss word in the dictionary, every poker hand in the deck and every whisky label in the distillery, but he can't even write his name. Can you?" he says to me.

"I don't need to write my name down," I said. "I can remember in my mind who I am."

"You're twelve years old," Walter Ewell said. "Man to man now, how many days in your life did you ever spend in school?"

"He ain't got time to go to school," Willy Legate said. "What's the use in going to school from September to middle of November, when he'll have to quit then to come in here and do Ernest's hearing for him? And what's the use in going back to school in January, when in jest eleven months it will be November fifteenth again and he'll have to start all over telling Ernest which way the dogs went?"

"Well, stop looking into my hand, anyway," Roth Edmonds said.

"What's that? What's that?" Mister Ernest said. He wore his listening button in his ear all the time, but he never brought the battery to camp with him because the cord would bound to get snagged ever time we run through a thicket.

"Willy says for me to go to bed!" I hollered.

"Don't you never call nobody 'mister'?" Willy said.

"I call Mister Ernest 'mister,' " I said.

"All right," Mister Ernest said. "Go to bed then. I don't need you."

"That ain't no lie," Willy said. "Deaf or no deaf, he can hear a fifty-dollar raise if you don't even move your lips."

So I went to bed, and after a while Mister Ernest come in and I wanted to tell him again how big them horns looked even half a quarter away in the river. Only I would 'a' had to holler, and the only time Mister Ernest agreed he couldn't hear was when we would be setting on

Dan, waiting for me to point which way the dogs was going. So we jest laid down, and it wasn't no time Simon was beating the bottom of the dishpan with the spoon, hollering, "Raise up and get your four-o'clock coffee!" and I crossed the river in the dark this time, with the lantern, and fed Dan and Roth Edmondziz horse. It was going to be a fine day, cold and bright; even in the dark I could see the white frost on the leaves and bushes—jest exactly the kind of day that big old son of a gun laying up there in that brake would like to run.

Then we et, and set the stand-holder across for Uncle Ike McCaslin to put them on the stands where he thought they ought to be, because he was the oldest one in camp. He had been hunting deer in these woods for about a hundred years, I reckon, and if anybody would know where a buck would pass, it would be him. Maybe with a big old buck like this one, that had been running the woods for what would amount to a hundred years in a deer's life, too, him and Uncle Ike would sholy manage to be at the same place at the same time this morning—provided, of course, he managed to git away from me and Mister Ernest on the jump. Because me and Mister Ernest was going to git him.

Then me and Mister Ernest and Roth Edmonds sent the dogs over, with Simon holding Eagle and the other old dogs on leash because the young ones, the puppies, wasn't going nowhere until Eagle let them, nohow. Then me and Mister Ernest and Roth saddled up, and Mister Ernest got up and I handed him up his pump gun and let Dan's bridle go for him to git rid of the spell of bucking he had to git shut of ever morning until Mister Ernest hit him between the ears with the gun barrel. Then Mister Ernest loaded the gun and give me the stirrup, and I got up behind him and we taken the fire road up toward the bayou, the four big dogs dragging Simon along in front with his single-barrel britchloader slung on a piece of plow line across his back, and the puppies moiling along in ever'body's way. It was light now and it was going to be jest fine; the east already yellow for the sun and our breaths smoking in the cold still bright air until the sun would come up and warm it, and a little skim of ice in the ruts, and ever leaf and twig and switch and even the frozen clods frosted over, waiting to sparkle like a rainbow when the sun finally come up and hit them. Until all my insides felt light and strong as a balloon, full of that light cold strong air, so that it seemed to me like I couldn't even feel the horse's back I was straddle of—jest the hot strong muscles moving under the hot strong skin, setting up there without no weight atall, so that when old Eagle struck and jumped, me and Dan and Mister Ernest would go jest like a bird, not even touching the ground. It was jest fine. When that big old buck got killed today, I knowed that even if he had put it off another ten years, he couldn't 'a' picked a better one.

And sho enough, as soon as we come to the bayou we seen his foot in the mud where he had come up out of the river last night, spread in the soft mud like a cow's foot, big as a cow's, big as a mule's, with Eagle and the other dogs laying into the leash rope now until Mister Ernest told me to jump down and help Simon hold them. Because me and Mister Ernest knowed exactly where he would be

—a little canebrake island in the middle of the bayou, where he could lay up until whatever doe or little deer the dogs had happened to jump could go up or down the bayou in either direction and take the dogs on away, so he could steal out and creep back down the bayou to the river and swim it, and leave the country like he always done the day the season opened.

Which is jest what we never aimed for him to do this time. So we left Roth on his horse to cut him off and turn him over Uncle Ike's standers if he tried to slip back down the bayou, and me and Simon, with the leashed dogs, walked on up the bayou until Mister Ernest on the horse said it was fur enough; then turned up into the woods about half a quarter above the brake because the wind was going to be south this morning when it riz, and turned down toward the brake, and Mister Ernest give the word to cast them, and we slipped the leash and Mister Ernest give me the stirrup again and I got up.

Old Eagle had done already took off because he knowed where that old son of a gun would be laying as good as we did, not making no racket atall yet, but jest boring on through the buck vines with the other dogs trailing along behind him, and even Dan seemed to know about that buck, too, beginning to souple up and jump a little through the vines, so that I taken my holt on Mister Ernest's belt already before the time had come for Mister Ernest to touch him. Because when we got strung out, going fast behind a deer, I wasn't on Dan's back much of the time nohow, but mostly jest strung out from my holt on Mister

Ernest's belt, so that Willy Legate said that when we was going through the woods fast, it looked like Mister Ernest had a boy-size pair of empty overalls blowing out of his hind pocket.

So it wasn't even a strike, it was a jump. Eagle must 'a' walked right up behind him or maybe even stepped on him while he was laying there still thinking it was day after tomorrow. Eagle jest throwed his head back and up and said, "There he goes," and we even heard the buck crashing through the first of the cane. Then all the other dogs was hollering behind him, and Dan give a squat to jump, but it was against the curb this time, not jest the snaffle, and Mister Ernest let him down into the bayou and swung him around the brake and up the other bank. Only he never had to say, "Which way?" because I was already pointing past his shoulder, freshening my holt on the belt jest as Mister Ernest touched Dan with that big old rusty spur on his nigh heel, because when Dan felt it he would go off jest like a stick of dynamite, straight through whatever he could bust and over or under what he couldn't, over it like a bird or under it crawling on his knees like a mole or a big coon, with Mister Ernest still on him because he had the saddle to hold on to, and me still there because I had Mister Ernest to hold on to; me and Mister Ernest not riding him, but jest going along with him, provided we held on. Because when the jump come, Dan never cared who else was there neither; I believe to my soul he could 'a' cast and run them dogs by hisself, without me or Mister Ernest or Simon or nobody.

That's what he done. He had to; the dogs was already almost out of hearing. Eagle must 'a' been looking right up that big son of a gun's tail until he finally decided he better git on out of there. And now they must 'a' been getting pretty close to Uncle Ike's standers, and Mister Ernest reined Dan back and held him, squatting and bouncing and trembling like a mule having his tail roached, while we listened for the shots. But never none come, and I hollered to Mister Ernest we better go on while I could still hear the dogs, and he let Dan off, but still there wasn't no shots, and now we knowed the racc had done already passed the standers, like that old son of a gun actually was a hant, like Simon and the other field hands said he was, and we busted out of a thicket, and sho enough there was Uncle Ike and Willy standing beside his foot in a soft patch.

"He got through us all," Uncle Ike said. "I don't know how he done it. I just had a glimpse of him. He looked big as a elephant, with a rack on his head you could cradle a yellin' calf in. He went right on down the ridge. You better get on, too; that Hog Bayou camp might not miss him."

So I freshened my holt and Mister Ernest touched Dan again. The ridge run due south; it was clear of vines and bushes so we could go fast, into the wind, too, because it had riz now, and now the sun was up, too; though I hadn't had time to notice it, bright and strong and level through the woods, shining and sparking like a rainbow on the frosted leaves. So we would hear the dogs again any time now as the wind got up; we could make time now, but still holding Dan back to a canter, because it was either going to be quick, when he got down to the standers from that Hog Bayou camp eight miles below ourn, or a long time, in case he got by them, too. And sho enough, after a while we heard the dogs; we was walking Dan now to let him blow a while, and we heard them, the sound coming faint up the wind, not running now, but trailing because the big son of a gun had decided a good piece back, probably, to put a end to this foolishness, and picked hisself up and soupled out and put about a mile between hisself and the dogs—until he run up on them other standers from that camp below. I could almost see him stopped behind a bush, peeping out and saying, "What's this? What's this? Is this whole durn country full of folks this morning?" Then looking back over his shoulder at where old Eagle and the others was hollering along after him while he decided how much time he had to decide what to do next.

Except he almost shaved it too fine. We heard the shots; it sounded like a war. Old Eagle must 'a' been looking right up his tail again and he had to bust on through the best way he could. "Pow, pow, pow, pow" and then "Pow, pow, pow, pow," like it must 'a' been three or four ganged right up on him before he had time even to swerve, and me hollering, "No! No! No! No!" because he was ourn. It was our beans and oats he et and our brake he laid in; we had been watching him every year, and it was like we had raised him, to be killed at last on our jump, in front of our dogs, by some strangers that would probably try to beat the dogs off and drag him away before we could even git a piece of the meat.

"Shut up and listen," Mister Ernest said. So I done it and we could hear the dogs; not just the others, but Eagle, too, not trailing no scent now and not baying no downed meat neither, but running hot on sight long after the shooting was over. I jest had time to freshen my holt. Yes, sir, they was running on sight. Like Willy Legate would say, if Eagle jest had a drink of whisky he would ketch that deer; going on, done already gone when we broke out of the thicket and seen the fellers that had done the shooting, five or six of them, squatting and crawling around, looking at the ground and the bushes, like maybe if they looked hard enough, spots of blood would bloom out on the stalks and leaves like frogstools or hawberries, with old Eagle still in hearing and still telling them that what blood they found wasn't coming out of nothing in front of him.

"Have any luck, boys?" Mister Ernest said.

"I think I hit him," one of them said. "I know I did. We're hunting blood now."

"Well, when you find him, blow your horn and I'll come back and tote him in to camp for you," Mister Ernest said.

So we went on, going fast now because the race was almost out of hearing again, going fast, too, like not jest the buck, but the dogs, too, had took a new leash on life from all the excitement and shooting.

We was in strange country now because we never had to run this fur before, we had always killed before now; now we had come to Hog Bayou that runs into the river a good fifteen miles below our camp. It had water in it, not to mention a mess of down trees and logs and such, and

Mister Ernest checked Dan again, saying, "Which way?"
I could just barely hear them, off to the east a little, like the
old son of a gun had give up the idea of Vicksburg or New
Orleans, like he first seemed to have, and had decided to
have a look at Alabama, maybe, since he was already up
and moving; so I pointed and we turned up the bayou hunting for a crossing, and maybe we could 'a' found one, except that I reckon Mister Ernest decided we never had
time to wait.

We come to a place where the bayou had narrowed
down to about twelve or fifteen feet, and Mister Ernest
said, "Look out, I'm going to touch him" and done it; I didn't
even have time to freshen my holt when we was already in
the air, and then I seen the vine—it was a loop of grapevine nigh as big as my wrist, looping down right across the
middle of the bayou—and I thought he seen it, too, and
was jest waiting to grab it and fling it up over our heads to
go under it, and I know Dan seen it because he even
ducked his head to jump under it. But Mister Ernest never
seen it atall until it skun back along Dan's neck and hooked
under the head of the saddle horn, us flying on through
the air, the loop of the vine gitting tighter and tighter until
something somewhere was going to have to give. It was the
saddle girth. It broke, and Dan going on and scrabbling up
the other bank bare nekkid except for the bridle, and me
and Mister Ernest and the saddle, Mister Ernest still setting
in the saddle holding the gun, and me still holding onto
Mister Ernest's belt, hanging in the air over the bayou in
the tightened loop of that vine like in the drawed-back

loop of a big rubber-banded slingshot, until it snapped
back and shot us back across the bayou and flang us clear,
me still holding onto Mister Ernest's belt and on the bottom
now, so that when we lit I would 'a' had Mister Ernest and
the saddle both on top of me if I hadn't clumb fast around
the saddle and up Mister Ernest's side, so that when we
landed, it was the saddle first, then Mister Ernest, and me
on top, until I jumped up, and Mister Ernest still laying
there with jest the white rim of his eyes showing.

"Mister Ernest!" I hollered, and then clumb down to
the bayou and scooped my cap full of water and clumb
back and throwed it in his face, and he opened his eyes and
laid there on the saddle cussing me.

"God dawg it," he said, "why didn't you stay behind
where you started out?"

"You was the biggest!" I said. "You would 'a' mashed
me flat!"

"What do you think you done to me?" Mister Ernest
said. "Next time, if you can't stay where you start out,
jump clear. Don't climb up on top of me no more. You
hear?"

"Yes, sir," I said.

So he got up then, still cussing and holding his back, and
clumb down to the water and dipped some in his hand
onto his face and neck and dipped some more up and drunk
it, and I drunk some, too, and clumb back and got the
saddle and the gun, and we crossed the bayou on the down
logs. If we could jest ketch Dan; not that he would have
went them fifteen miles back to camp, because, if anything,

he would have went on by hisself to try to help Eagle ketch that buck. But he was about fifty yards away, eating buck vines, so I brought him back, and we taken Mister Ernest's galluses and my belt and the whang leather loop off Mister Ernest's horn and tied the saddle back on Dan. It didn't look like much, but maybe it would hold.

"Provided you don't let me jump him through no more grapevines without hollering first," Mister Ernest said.

"Yes, sir," I said. "I'll holler first next time—provided you'll holler a little quicker when you touch him next time, too." But it was all right; we jest had to be a little easy getting up. "Now which-a-way?" I said. Because we couldn't hear nothing now, after wasting all this time. And this was new country, sho enough. It had been cut over and growed up in thickets we couldn't 'a' seen over even standing up on Dan.

But Mister Ernest never even answered. He jest turned Dan along the bank of the bayou where it was a little more open and we could move faster again, soon as Dan and us got used to that homemade cinch strop and got a little confidence in it. Which jest happened to be east, or so I thought then, because I never paid no particular attention to east then because the sun—I don't know where the morning had went, but it was gone, the morning and the frost, too—was up high now, even if my insides had told me it was past dinnertime.

And then we heard him. No, that's wrong; what we heard was shots. And that was when we realized how fur we had come, because the only camp we knowed about in that direction was the Hollyknowe camp, and Holly-knowe was exactly twenty-eight miles from Van Dorn, where me and Mister Ernest lived—jest the shots, no dogs nor nothing. If old Eagle was still behind him and the buck was still alive, he was too wore out now to even say, "Here he comes."

"Don't touch him!" I hollered. But Mister Ernest remembered that cinch strop, too, and he jest let Dan off the snaffle. And Dan heard them shots, too, picking his way through the thickets, hopping the vines and logs when he could and going under them when he couldn't. And sho enough, it was jest like before—two or three men squatting and creeping among the bushes, looking for blood that Eagle had done already told them wasn't there. But we never stopped this time, jest trotting on by with Dan hopping and dodging among the brush and vines dainty as a dancer. Then Mister Ernest swung Dan until we was going due north.

"Wait!" I hollered. "Not this way."

But Mister Ernest jest turned his face back over his shoulder. It looked tired, too, and there was a smear of mud on it where that ere grapevine had snatched him off the horse.

"Don't you know where he's heading?" he said. "He's done done his part, give everybody a fair open shot at him, and now he's going home, back to that brake in our bayou. He ought to make it exactly at dark."

And that's what he was doing. We went on. It didn't matter to hurry now. There wasn't no sound nowhere; it was that time in the early afternoon in November when don't nothing move or cry, not even birds, the peckerwoods and yellowhammers and jays, and it seemed to me like I could see all three of us—me and Mister Ernest and Dan— and Eagle, and the other dogs, and that big old buck, moving through the quiet woods in the same direction, headed for the same place, not running now but walking, that had all run the fine race the best we knowed how, and all three of us now turned like on a agreement to walk back home, not together in a bunch because we didn't want to worry or tempt one another, because what we had all three spent this morning doing was no play-acting jest for fun, but was serious, and all three of us was still what we was—that old buck that had to run, not because he was skeered, but because running was what he done the best and was proudest at; and Eagle and the dogs that chased him, not because they hated or feared him, but because that was the thing they done the best and was proudest at; and me and Mister Ernest and Dan, that run him not because we wanted his meat, which would be too tough to eat anyhow, or his head to hang on a wall, but because now we could go back and work hard for eleven months making a crop, so we would have the right to come back here next November—all three of us going back home now, peaceful and separate, but still side by side, until next year, next time.

Then we seen him for the first time. We was out of the cut-over now; we could even 'a' cantered, except that all three of us was long past that, and now you could tell where west was because the sun was already halfway down it. So we was walking, too, when we come on the dogs—

the puppies and one of the old ones—played out, laying in a little wet swag, panting, jest looking up at us when we passed, but not moving when we went on. Then we come to a long open glade, you could see about half a quarter, and we seen the three other old dogs and about a hundred yards ahead of them Eagle, all walking, not making no sound; and then suddenly, at the fur end of the glade, the buck hisself getting up from where he had been resting for the dogs to come up, getting up without no hurry, big, big as a mule, tall as a mule, and turned without no hurry still, and the white underside of his tail for a second or two more before the thicket taken him.

It might 'a' been a signal, a good-bye, a farewell. Still walking, we passed the other three old dogs in the middle of the glade, laying down, too, now jest where they was when the buck vanished, and not trying to get up neither when we passed; and still that hundred yards ahead of them, Eagle, too, not laying down, because he was still on his feet, but his legs was spraddled and his head was down; maybe jest waiting until we was out of sight of his shame, his eyes saying plain as talk when we passed, "I'm sorry, boys, but this here is all."

Mister Ernest stopped Dan. "Jump down and look at his feet," he said.

"Ain't nothing wrong with his feet," I said. "It's his wind has done give out."

"Jump down and look at his feet," Mister Ernest said.

So I done it, and while I was stooping over Eagle I could hear the pump gun go, "Snick-cluck. Snick-cluck. Snick-cluck" three times, except that I never thought nothing then. Maybe he was jest running the shells through to be sho it would work when we seen him again or maybe to make sho they was all buckshot. Then I got up again, and we went on, still walking; a little west of north now, because when we seen his white flag that second or two before the thicket hid it, it was on a beeline for that notch in the bayou. And it was evening, too, now. The wind had done dropped and there was a edge to the air and the sun jest touched the tops of the trees now, except jest now and then, when it found a hole to come almost level through onto the ground. And he was taking the easiest way, too, now, going straight as he could. When we seen his foot in the soft places he was running for a while at first after his rest. But soon he was walking, too, like he knowed, too, where Eagle and the dogs was.

And then we seen him again. It was the last time—a thicket, with the sun coming through a hole onto it like a searchlight. He crashed jest once; then he was standing there broadside to us, not twenty yards away, big as a statue and red as gold in the sun, and the sun sparking on the tips of his horns—they was twelve of them—so that he looked like he had twelve lighted candles branched around his head, standing there looking at us while Mister Ernest raised the gun and aimed at his neck, and the gun went, "Click. Snick-cluck. Click. Snick-cluck. Click. Snick-cluck" three times, and Mister Ernest still holding the gun aimed while the buck turned and give one long bound, the white underside of his tail like a blaze of fire, too, until the thicket and the shadows put it out; and Mister Ernest laid the gun slow and gentle back across the saddle in front of him, saying quiet and peaceful, and not much louder than jest breathing, "God dawg. God dawg."

Then he jogged me with his elbow and we got down, easy and careful because of that ere cinch strop, and he reached into his vest and taken out one of the cigars. It was busted where I had fell on it, I reckon, when we hit the ground. He throwed it away and taken out the other one. It was busted, too, so he bit off a hunk of it to chew and throwed the rest away. And now the sun was gone even from the tops of the trees and there wasn't nothing left but a big red glare in the west.

"Don't worry," I said. "I ain't going to tell them you forgot to load your gun. For that matter, they don't need to know we ever seed him."

"Much oblige," Mister Ernest said. There wasn't going to be no moon tonight neither, so he taken the compass off the whang leather loop in his buttonhole and handed me the gun and set the compass on a stump and stepped back and looked at it. "Jest about the way we're headed now," he said, and taken the gun from me and opened it and put one shell in the britch and taken up the compass, and I taken Dan's reins and we started, with him in front with the compass in his hand.

And after a while it was full dark; Mister Ernest would have to strike a match ever now and then to read the compass, until the stars come out good and we could pick out one to follow, because I said, "How fur do you reckon it

is?" and he said, "A little more than one box of matches."
So we used a star when we could, only we couldn't see it
all the time because the woods was too dense and we would
git a little off until he would have to spend another match.
And now it was good and late, and he stopped and said,
"Get on the horse."

"I ain't tired," I said.

"Get on the horse," he said. "We don't want to spoil
him."

Because he had been a good feller ever since I had
knowed him, which was even before that day two years
ago when maw went off with the Vicksburg roadhouse
feller and the next day pap didn't come home neither, and
on the third one Mister Ernest rid Dan up to the door of
the cabin on the river he let us live in, so pap could work
his piece of land and run his fish line, too, and said, "Put
that gun down and come on here and climb up behind."

So I got in the saddle even if I couldn't reach the stirrups,
and Mister Ernest taken the reins and I must 'a' went to
sleep, because the next thing I knowed a buttonhole of
my lumberjack was tied to the saddle horn with that ere
whang cord off the compass, and it was good and late now
and we wasn't fur, because Dan was already smelling water,
the river. Or maybe it was the feed lot itself he smelled,
because we struck the fire road not a quarter below it, and
soon I could see the river, too, with the white mist laying
on it soft and still as cotton. Then the lot, home; and up
yonder in the dark, not no piece akchully, close enough to
hear us unsaddling and shucking corn prob'ly, and sholy

close enough to hear Mister Ernest blowing his horn at the dark camp for Simon to come in the boat and git us, that old buck in his brake in the bayou; home, too, resting, too, after the hard run, waking hisself now and then, dreaming of dogs behind him or maybe it was the racket we was making would wake him, but not neither of them for more than jest a little while before sleeping again.

Then Mister Ernest stood on the bank blowing until Simon's lantern went bobbing down into the mist; then we clumb down to the landing and Mister Ernest blowed again now and then to guide Simon, until we seen the lantern in the mist, and then Simon and the boat; only it looked like ever time I set down and got still, I went back to sleep, because Mister Ernest was shaking me again to git out and climb the bank into the dark camp, until I felt a bed against my knees and tumbled into it.

Then it was morning, tomorrow; it was all over now until next November, next year, and we could come back. Uncle Ike and Willy and Walter and Roth and the rest of them had come in yestiddy, soon as Eagle taken the buck out of hearing and they knowed that deer was gone, to pack up and be ready to leave this morning for Yoknapatawpha, where they lived, until it would be November again and they could come back again.

So, as soon as we et breakfast, Simon run them back up the river in the big boat to where they left their cars and pickups, and now it wasn't nobody but jest me and Mister Ernest setting on the bench against the kitchen wall in the sun; Mister Ernest smoking a cigar—a whole one this time that Dan hadn't had no chance to jump him through a grapevine and bust. He hadn't washed his face neither where that vine had throwed him into the mud. But that was all right, too; his face usually did have a smudge of mud or tractor grease or beard stubble on it, because he wasn't jest a planter; he was a farmer, he worked as hard as ara one of his hands and tenants—which is why I knowed from the very first that we would git along, that I wouldn't have no trouble with him and he wouldn't have no trouble with me, from that very first day when I woke up and maw had done gone off with that Vicksburg road-house feller without even waiting to cook breakfast, and the next morning pap was gone, too, and it was almost night the next day when I heard a horse coming up and I taken the gun that I had already throwed a shell into the britch when pap never come home last night, and stood in the door while Mister Ernest rid up and said, "Come on. Your paw ain't coming back neither."

"You mean he give me to you?" I said.

"Who cares?" he said. "Come on. I brought a lock for the door. We'll send the pickup back tomorrow for whatever you want."

So I come home with him and it was all right, it was jest fine—his wife had died about three years ago—without no women to worry us or take off in the middle of the night with a durn Vicksburg roadhouse jake without even waiting to cook breakfast. And we would go home this afternoon, too, but not jest yet; we always stayed one more day after the others left because Uncle Ike always left

what grub they hadn't et, and the rest of the homemade
corn whisky he drunk and that town whisky of Roth Edmondziz he called Scotch that smelled like it come out of a
old bucket of roof paint; setting in the sun for one more
day before we went back home to git ready to put in next
year's crop of cotton and oats and beans and hay; and
across the river yonder, behind the wall of trees where the
big woods started, that old buck laying up today in the
sun, too—resting today, too, without nobody to bother
him until next November.

So at least one of us was glad it would be eleven months
and two weeks before he would have to run that fur that
fast again. So he was glad of the very same thing we was
sorry of, and so all of a sudden I thought about how maybe
planting and working and then harvesting oats and cotton
and beans and hay wasn't jest something me and Mister
Ernest done three hundred and fifty-one days to fill in the
time until we could come back hunting again, but it was
something we had to do, and do honest and good during
the three hundred and fifty-one days, to have the right to
come back into the big woods and hunt for the other fourteen; and the fourteen days that old buck run in front of
dogs wasn't jest something to fill his time until the three
hundred and fifty-one when he didn't have to, but the running and the risking in front of guns and dogs was something he had to do for fourteen days to have the right not
to be bothered for the other three hundred and fifty-one.
And so the hunting and the farming wasn't two different
things atall—they was jest the other side of each other.

"Yes," I said. "All we got to do now is put in that next year's crop. Then November won't be no time away atall."

"You ain't going to put in the crop next year," Mister Ernest said. "You're going to school."

So at first I didn't even believe I had heard him. "What?" I said. "Me? Go to school?"

"Yes," Mister Ernest said. "You must make something out of yourself."

"I am," I said. "I'm doing it now. I'm going to be a hunter and a farmer like you."

"No," Mister Ernest said. "That ain't enough any more. Time was when all a man had to do was just farm eleven and a half months, and hunt the other half. But not now. Now just to belong to the farming business and the hunting business ain't enough. You got to belong to the business of mankind."

"Mankind?" I said.

"Yes," Mister Ernest said. "So you're going to school. Because you got to know why. You can belong to the farming and hunting business and you can learn the difference between what's right and what's wrong, and do right. And that used to be enough—just to do right. But not now. You got to know why it's right and why it's wrong, and be able to tell the folks that never had no chance to learn it; teach them how to do what's right, not just because they know it's right, but because they know now why it's right because you just showed them, told them, taught them why. So you're going to school."

"It's because you been listening to that durn Will Legate and Walter Ewell!" I said.

"No," Mister Ernest said.

"Yes!" I said. "No wonder you missed that buck yestiddy, taking ideas from the very fellers that let him git away, after me and you had run Dan and the dogs durn night clean to death! Because you never even missed him! You never forgot to load that gun! You had done already unloaded it a purpose! I heard you!"

"All right, all right," Mister Ernest said. "Which would you rather have? His bloody head and hide on the kitchen floor yonder and half his meat in a pickup truck on the way to Yoknapatawpha County, or him with his head and hide and meat still together over yonder in that brake, waiting for next November for us to run him again?"

"And git him, too," I said. "We won't even fool with no Willy Legate and Walter Ewell next time."

"Maybe," Mister Ernest said.

"Yes," I said.

"Maybe," Mister Ernest said. "The best word in our language, the best of all. That's what mankind keeps going on: Maybe. The best days of his life ain't the ones when he said 'Yes' beforehand: they're the ones when all he knew to say was 'Maybe.' He can't say 'Yes' until afterward because he not only don't know it until then, he don't want to know 'Yes' until then. . . . Step in the kitchen and make me a toddy. Then we'll see about dinner."

"All right," I said. I got up. "You want some of Uncle Ike's corn or that town whisky of Roth Edmondziz?"

"Can't you say Mister Roth or Mister Edmonds?" Mister Ernest said.

"Yes, sir," I said. "Well, which do you want? Uncle Ike's corn or that ere stuff of Roth Edmondziz?"

The old hunter said:

*soon we will enter the woods. It is not new to me, since
I have been doing it each November for over seventy
years—this last hill, at the foot of which the rich unbroken
alluvial flatness begins as the sea begins at the base of
its cliffs, dissolving away beneath the unhurried November
rain as the seat itself dissolves away.*

*In the old days we came in wagons: the guns, the
bedding, the dogs, the food, the whisky; the young men
then who could drive all night and all the next day in the
cold rain and pitch a camp in the rain and sleep in wet
blankets and rise at daylight the next morning and hunt.
There had been bear then. A man shot a doe or a fawn
as quickly as he did a buck, and in the afternoons we shot
wild turkey with pistols to test our stalking skill and aim,
feeding all but the breasts to the dogs. But that time is*

gone now. Now we go in cars, driving faster and faster each year because the roads are better and the distance greater, the Big Woods where game still runs drawing yearly inward as my life is doing, until now I am the last of those who once made the trip in wagons without feeling it; and now those who accompany me are the sons and even grandsons of the men who rode for twenty-four hours in rain or sleet behind the steaming mules. They call me "Uncle Ike" now and few of them even care how much past eighty I am: all they care is what I myself know too: that I probably no longer have any business making this trip, even by car.

In fact, each time now, on the first night in camp, lying aching and unable to sleep in the harsh blankets, my blood only faintly warmed by the single whisky-and-water which I allow myself, I tell myself that this will be my last one. But I would stand that trip—I still shoot about as well as I ever did, still kill almost as much of the game I see as I ever killed; I have forgotten, if I ever kept a count, of how many bear or deer my gun has scored— and the warmth, heat, of next summer would restore me, renew me. Then November; again in the car with two or three of the sons or even grandsons of men whom I had taught to distinguish between not only the prints left by a buck or a doe, but between the sound they made moving, I would look ahead beyond the jerking windshield wiper and see the land flatten and dissolve away beneath the *rain as the sea itself does, and say, "Well, boys, there it is again."*

Because to them, there it was. They are too recent to have any past in the history of its change; to them, it has simply moved intact in geography. Only to me has it exposed geography as the dying of a body exposes its defenseless mortality. At first there had been only the old towns along the River and the old towns along the hills, from each of which the planters with their gangs of slaves and then of hired laborers advanced to wrest from the cane and gum and cypress and holly and oak, the cotton patches which as the years passed became fields and then plantations; the very paths made by bear and deer and panther become the roads and highways linking the little towns still bearing the names of the old hunting stands: Panther Burn, Bucksnort, Bear Gun.

Now a man has to drive two hundred miles to find enough woods to harbor game worth hunting. Now the land lies open from hills to levee, standing horseman-tall in cotton for the world's looms, right up to the doorsteps of the Negroes who work it and the white men who own it. Because it is too rich for anything else, too rich and strong to have remained wilderness—land so rich and strong that, as those who live in and by it say, it exhausts the life of a dog in one year, a mule in five and a man in twenty—a land where neon flashes past us in the gray rain from the little countless towns and countless shining

this-year's automobiles, the plumb-straight roads
stringing like endless beads the tremendous cotton-gins,
all looking brand-new as though clapped together
yesterday from numbered sections of sheet-iron, like the
houses, the homes themselves, since no man, no matter
how many times a millionaire, would build more than a
simple roof and walls to camp in while he grows still
richer in this land where every decade or so even the
dyked streams will overflow up to the second storey—
this land across which comes now not the scream of
panther but the hooting of locomotives: trains of
incredible length and drawn by one engine, since there
are no grades anywhere except the dirt mounds of the old
precessors, used in their turn by Chickasaw and
Choctaw to sepulchre their fathers' bones; these gone
too now so that all which remains are the Indian names
on the little towns, usually pertaining to water:
Aluschaskuna, Tillatoba, Homochitto, Yazoo.

But even two hundred miles end in time, and now we
are on water: the river of our destination, the last highway
into the last of the Big Woods. We unload from the cars
and trucks, into the boats; the horses will follow the river
bank on to a point opposite camp, where they will be
swum across. It is my hand, though it has more than
eighty years, which coaxes and soothes them until,
backing and filling, trembling a little, they spring
scrambling down from the truck. It will be my hand again

later when we reach the camp site with two hours of daylight left. "You go over under that driest tree and set down," Will Legate tells me "—if you can find it. Me and these other young boys will ten' to this." But I am not tired yet. That will come later. Maybe it will not come at all this time, I think, as I have thought at this point each November for the last five or six of them. Maybe I will even go out on a stand in the morning too, I tell myself, knowing that I will not. Because it will not be the fatigue. It will be because I shall not sleep tonight but instead lie wakeful and peaceful on my cot amid the tent-filling snoring and the rain's whisper as I always do on this first night in camp, who dont have enough of them left now to waste one sleeping.

So in my streaming slicker I supervise the unloading of the boats—the tents, the stove, the bedding, the food for ourselves and the dogs and horses until there will be meat in camp. I dispatch two of the Negroes to cut firewood; we have the cook-tent raised and the stove up and a fire and supper cooking while the big tent is still being staked down and trenched. By then the horses have appeared on the other bank; again it is my hand (my voice first shouting across the rain at the other Negro, the boy, who is trying to beat the horses down into the river) on the lead ropes, no more weight than that and my voice drawing them down into the water, then holding them beside the moving boat with only their heads above the surface as though they actually are suspended from this frail and strengthless old man's grip, until they are once more up the bank.

Then the meal is ready. I have my one glass of thin whisky and water. Then we uncover, and, standing in the churned mud beneath the stretched tarpaulin, I say grace over the fried slabs of pork, the soft shapeless bread, the canned beans and molasses and coffee in the iron plates and cups—the town food we brought with us—then we cover ourselves and eat. "Eat it all up," I say. "I don't want a piece of town meat in camp after breakfast tomorrow. Then you boys will hunt. When I first started hunting in this bottom seventy years ago with old General Compson and Major de Spain and Walter's father and Roth's and Will's grandfathers, (and Boon Hogganbeck, the forty-year-old adolescent boy who killed the big old warp-footed bear with his bare hands and a pocket-knife) Major de Spain wouldn't allow but two pieces of foreign grub in his camp. That was one side of pork and one ham of beef. And not to eat for the first supper and breakfast either, but to save until along toward the end of the hunt when everybody would be so sick of bear meat and coon and venison we couldn't even bear to look at them."

"I thought Uncle Ike was going to say the pork and beef was for the dogs," Will Legate says. "But that's right; I remember. You just shot the dogs a mess of wild turkey when they burnt out on deer guts."

"There was game here then," Walter Ewell says.

"Not to mention they shot does," Will says.

"There's game here still," I say. "A good hunter can find it without shooting does either when the law says he shant. Remember that. And remember too why there had to be game laws at last."

"Meaning me and Walter and Will Legate," Roth Edmonds says.

"Meaning all of us," I say. "God created man and He created the world for him to live in; I reckon He created the kind of a world He would have wanted to live in if He had been a man—the ground to walk on, the Big Woods, the trees and the water, and the game to live in it. And maybe He didn't put the desire to hunt and kill game in man, but I reckon He knew it was going to be there, that man was going to teach himself that, since he wasn't quite God yet. So I reckon He foreknew man would follow and kill the game. I believe He said, So be it. I reckon He even foresaw the end. But He said, I will give him his chance, I will give him warning and foreknowledge too, along with the desire to follow and the power to slay. The woods and fields he ravages and the game he devastates will be the consequence and signature of his crime and guilt, and his punishment.— Bed time," I say; then to young Ash: "Breakfast at four o'clock, Ash, We want meat on the ground by sunup."

There is a good fire in the heater; the tent is already warm and is even beginning to dry out except for the mud

we had to set it up in. Young Ash has made my bed too
—the strong battered iron cot, the stained mattress
which was never quite soft enough, the worn,
often-washed blankets which as the years pass are less
and less warm enough. But the tent is warm; presently
when the kitchen tent is cleaned up and readied for
breakfast, Joseph, the young Negro, Ash's helper, will
come and make his bed down before the heater where he
can be roused from time to time to put in more wood.
So at least I will have comfort to lie awake in, which I
have known all the time that I shall do, being unable to
sleep this first night. Or maybe I dont want to sleep.
Maybe this is what I have come for. So, the spectacles
folded away in the worn case beneath the pillow where I
can find them, the lean old man's sapless body folded and
fitted easily into the worn old groove in the old mattress,
hands crossed on breast as if in rehearsal for that last
attitude of relinquishment and peace, I lie with my eyes
closed until the sounds of undressing have subsided and
the snoring begins. Then I open my eyes and lie looking
up at the motionless belly of rain-murmured canvas upon
which the glow of the heater fades slowly toward the
moment when Joseph will rouse and stoke it again.

We—the camp—had a house once, seventy and sixty
and even just forty years ago when the Big Woods were
only thirty miles from Jefferson and Major de Spain who
had been my father's cavalry commander in '61 and '2

and '3 and '4, and my cousin (cousin? my older brother,
my father too) brought me into the woods for the first
time. Old Sam Fathers was alive then, born in slavery of
a Negro girl and a Chickasaw chief, who had taught me
to shoot, not just when to shoot but when not to; such a
November dawn as tomorrow will be and old Sam led
me straight to the big cypress, knowing the buck would
pass there because something ran in Sam Fathers' blood
which ran in the buck's also, we standing there against
the tremendous trunk, Sam Fathers who owned the
seventy years then because then I owned only twelve of
them; and there was nothing save the dawn until suddenly
the buck was there, smoke-colored out of nothing,
beautiful, magnificent with speed: and Sam said, "Now.
Shoot quick and shoot slow": and the gun levelled rapidly
without haste as though of its own volition and will and
crashed and I walked to the buck lying still intact and
still in the attitude of that magnificent speed and bled it
with Sam's knife and Sam dipped his hands into the hot
blood and marked my face forever while I stood trying
not to tremble, humbly and with pride too though a boy
of twelve could not actually have phrased it: "I slew you;
my bearing must not shame your quitting life. My
conduct forever afterward must become your death." I
own a house in Jefferson. That is, it is recorded to me,
I pay taxes on it, it is specified as my domicile, since it
contains the impedimenta necessary for a human being

*to get through life with: stove, bed, spare clothing—
somewhere to store and keep the relics of human
mutation: the crushed now scentless rose or violet or field
daisy of first love, the grammar- or high-school medal,
the mounted head of the first stag. But it is not my home.
It is merely the way station in which I pass the time
waiting for November again. Because this is my home:
this tent with its muddy floor and the bed neither wide
enough nor soft enough nor even warm enough for the
old bones; my kin, the men whose ghosts alone still
companion me: De Spain and Compson and the old
Walter Ewell and Hogganbeck.*

    *Because this is my land. I can feel it, tremendous,
still primeval, looming, musing downward upon the tent,
the camp—this whole puny evanescent clutter of human
sojourn which after our two weeks will vanish, and in
another week will be completely healed, traceless in this
unmarked solitude. It is mine, though I have never owned
a foot of it, and never will. I have never wanted to, not
even after I saw that it is doomed, not even after I began
to watch it retreat year by year before the onslaught of
axe and saw and log-lines and then dynamite and plow.
Because there was never any one for me to acquire and
possess it from because it had belonged to no one man.
It belonged to all; we had only to use it well, humbly and
with pride. Then suddenly I know why I have never
wanted to own any of it, never wanted to arrest at least*

*that much of what man calls progress, measure my
longevity at least against that much of the wilderness's
ultimate fate. It is because there is just exactly enough of
it. It is as if I can see the two of us—myself and the
wilderness—as coevals, my own span as a hunter, a
woodsman, not contemporary with my own first breath
but instead transmitted to me, assumed by me gladly,
humbly, with joy and pride, from the old Major de Spain
and the old Sam Fathers who had taught me to hunt, the
two spans—mine and the wilderness's—running out
together, not toward oblivion, nothingness, but into a
dimension free of both time and space where once more
the untreed land warped and wrung to mathematical
squares of rank cotton for the frantic old-world people
to turn into shells to shoot at one another, would find
ample room for both—the names, the faces of the old
men I had known and loved and for a little while outlived,
moving again among the shades of the tall unaxed trees
and sightless brakes where the wild strong immortal
game ran forever before the tireless belling immortal
hounds, falling and rising phoenixlike to the soundless
guns—*

*I have been asleep. The lantern is lighted; outside in
the darkness the oldest Negro, old Isham, is beating a
spoon against a tin pan and crying, "Raise up and get yo
foa clock coffy. Raise up and get yo foa clock coffy," and
the tent is filled now with the sound of men dressing,*

and Will Legate's voice: "Get out of here now and let Uncle Ike sleep. If we wake him up, he'll insist on going out with us. And he ain't got any business in the woods this morning."

So I do not move, simulating sleep while they leave the tent. I listen to the breakfast sounds from beneath the stretched tarpaulin, and hear them depart—the horses, the dogs; the last voice dies away and there remain only the Negroes clearing breakfast away; presently I may even hear the first faint clear cry of the first hound, the strike dog, ring through the wet woods from where the buck bedded, and perhaps I will even go back to sleep again. Then the tent flap swings in and falls, something jolts against the foot of the cot and I open my eyes. It is Roth, Roth Edmonds, grandson of the McCaslin Edmonds who had been not just my cousin but my older brother and father too in the time when I had neither, carrying not the rifle which he had used ever since he had finally seen that a man with a steady eye and hand owed more to the bear or the buck than to shoot it with a blind handful of pellets, but a shotgun.

"Are you going to shoot that today?" I say.

"You said last night you want meat this morning," he says.

"Since when did you start having trouble getting meat with your rifle?" I say.

But he is already gone; the tent flap falls again and

*now there is only the murmur of the rain, the waft of
light and the cold wet smell of actual rain snatched,
jerked out of the tent again; I cry: "Roth! Wait!" But it
is too late, too late not just now, this morning, not even
yesterday, but already too late much longer ago than any
of these; I am trembling now, the blanket huddled to my
chin, my hands crossed on my breast as though I hoped
to huddle for warmth even within their frail
circumscription. It is cold; I lie shaking faintly and
steadily in it, rigid save for the shaking, until—I don't
know how much later, since long enough is already
too late—the flap lifts again and this time Legate almost
scuttles in, almost furtive.*

"What?" I say.

*"A tarpaulin," Legate says. "We got a deer on the
ground."*

*"Why a tarpaulin for a dead deer?" I say. Then I
answer it myself: "Who killed it?" I say. "It was Roth,"
answering that too. "It was a doe."*

"I tried not to wake you," Legate says.

"All right," I say. "Bring it in."

"All of it?" Legate says.

"All of it?" I say. "You mean he shot two of them?"

"That other one is pretty old and tough," Legate says.

*"Bring her in!" I say. "Feed her to the dogs if you like.
But don't let her lay out there in the woods."*

"All right, all right," Legate says. Then he is gone too

and now I can lie again in the empty tent, shaking, but only with the cold, since there is nothing left now ponderable enough to cause a man to tremble: only to remember and to grieve of this land which man has deswamped and denuded and deriverved in two generations so that white men can own plantations and commute every night to Memphis, and black men own plantations and ride in jim crow cars to Chicago to live in millionaires' mansions on Lakeshore Drive; this land where white men rent farms and live like niggers and Negroes crop on shares and live like animals; where cotton grows man-tall in the very cracks in the sidewalk, mortgaged before it is even planted and sold and the money spent before it is ever harvested, and usury and mortgage and bankruptcy and measureless wealth all breed and spawn together until no man has time to say which one is which, or cares. . . .

This land, said the old hunter. No wonder the ruined woods I used to know don't cry for retribution. The very people who destroyed them will accomplish their revenge.

VINTAGE INTERNATIONAL

POSSESSION
by A. S. Byatt

An intellectual mystery and a triumphant love story of a pair of young scholars researching the lives of two Victorian poets.

"Gorgeously written...dazzling...a tour de force."

—*The New York Times Book Review*

Fiction/Literature/0-679-73590-9

THE STRANGER
by Albert Camus

Through the story of an ordinary man who unwittingly gets drawn into a senseless murder, Camus explores what he termed "the nakedness of man faced with the absurd."

Fiction/Literature/0-679-72020-0

INVISIBLE MAN
by Ralph Ellison

This searing record of a black man's journey through contemporary America reveals, in Ralph Ellison's words, "the sheer rhetorical challenge involved in communicating across our barriers of race and religion, class, color and region."

"The greatest American novel in the second half of the twentieth century...the classic representation of American black experience." —R.W. D. Lewis

Fiction/Literature/0-679-72313-7

THE REMAINS OF THE DAY
by Kazuo Ishiguro

A profoundly compelling portrait of the perfect English butler and of his fading, insular world in postwar England.

"One of the best books of the year." —*The New York Times Book Review*

Fiction/Literature/0-679-73172-5

ALL THE PRETTY HORSES
by Cormac McCarthy

At sixteen, John Grady Cole finds himself at the end of a long line of Texas ranchers, cut off from the only life he has ever imagined for himself. With two companions, he sets off for Mexico on a sometimes idyllic, sometimes comic journey, to a place where dreams are paid for in blood.

"A book of remarkable beauty and strength, the work of a master in perfect command of his medium." —*Washington Post Book World*

Winner of the National Book Award for Fiction
Fiction/Literature/0-679-74439-8

THE ENGLISH PATIENT
by Michael Ondaatje

During the final moments of World War II, four damaged people come together in a deserted Italian villa. As their stories unfold, a complex tapestry of image and emotion, recollection and observation is woven, leaving them inextricably connected by the brutal, improbable circumstances of war.

"It seduces and beguiles us with its many-layered mysteries, its brilliantly taut and lyrical prose, its tender regard for its characters." —*Newsday*

Winner of the Booker Prize
Fiction/Literature/0-679-74520-3

LOLITA
by Vladimir Nabokov

The famous and controversial novel that tells the story of the aging Humbert Humbert's obsessive, devouring, and doomed passion for the nymphet Dolores Haze.

"The only convincing love story of our century." —*Vanity Fair*

Fiction/Literature/0-679-72316-1

OPERATION SHYLOCK
by Philip Roth

In this tour de force of fact and fiction, Philip Roth meets a man who may or may not be Philip Roth. Because *someone* with that name has been touring the State of Israel, promoting a bizarre exodus in reverse, and it is up to Roth to stop him—even if that means impersonating his impersonator.

"A diabolically clever, engaging work...Roth is so splendidly convincing...that the result is a kind of dizzying exhilaration." —*Boston Globe*

Fiction/Literature/0-679-75029-0

Amadeus Music 332 fore 772-8414
CD Authority mill Creek Shopping Ctr. S Port. 799-983

V I N T A G E   I N T E R N A T I O N A L